Lillian Duncan

Trapped
COPYRIGHT 2019 by Lillian Duncan

Contact Information: titleadmin@pelicanbookgroup.com

Cover Art by *Nicola Martinez*

Harbourlight Books, a division of Pelican Ventures, LLC
www.pelicanbookgroup.com PO Box 1738 *Aztec, NM * 87410

Harbourlight Books sail and mast logo is a trademark of Pelican Ventures, LLC

Publishing History
First Harbourlight Edition, 2019
Paperback Edition ISBN 978-1-5223-0210-0
Electronic Edition ISBN 978-1-5223-0208-7
Published in the United States of America

Dedication

This and all I do is for God's glory.
Without the unfailing support of my husband, Ronny
Duncan, in more ways than I have space to write,
thank you for all you do.

What People are Saying…

GAME ON (2016)

Game On is a romantic-suspense story layered with intrigue that captivates the reader on the first page and doesn't let go till the last page is turned. Lillian Duncan adds one surprise turn after another to keep readers on the edge of their seat. I enjoyed reading this book and recommend it to all suspense lovers.

~ Jo Huddleston, author of the West Virginia Mountains series of sweet Southern historical romances

I have enjoyed every book I have read by this author, and I got this one as soon as it was released. I was not disappointed in this one. There is lots of suspense, romance, family secrets and faith which resulted in a story that I couldn't put down after I had started it.

~ Ann Lacey Ellison, reader

1

"Why are you doing this?" Her eyes were open. Not that it did any good since she was surrounded by complete darkness. With a madman.

"I thought you might want to play a game with me, Ange," came the whispered response. "Want to play with me?"

And then a sharp jab on the bottom of her foot.

She whimpered.

"Don't you like my game, Ange?"

Another sharp jab. On her shoulder this time. "How about it, Ange? Do you want to play, Ange?" came the whisper.

Each time he said her name, she cringed, knowing pain would follow. Before she could take another breath a knife scraped against her leg, leaving a trail of pain up to her knee. Probably blood, too. Not that she could see it.

"Stop it. Leave me alone." The words came out as a whisper even though she'd meant to yell them. "Why are you doing this to me?"

In answer, the room was flooded with light. Her eyes protested at the sudden change. She squinted at her captor as he came closer.

"Because I can." He bared his white teeth in what would probably pass for a smile in a different situation even as his eyes darkened with hatred. "Women like you think you have all the power because you're rich and beautiful. You think you can do what you want, then discard us like we're nothing. Well, who's nothing now, Ange? Who's the one in control?" He held up the knife as if to emphasize his words.

She stared up from the bed. Her hands and feet were tied to opposite bedposts. All she had on was a long T-shirt. The dirt was his. The blood was hers. "I never did anything to you. I don't even know you. Please...please...this...this...isn't right. Just let me go. Please."

His bright blue eyes glittered with hatred and excitement as he stared at her.

She wasn't sure what drove him to such horrible actions, but the man was evil incarnate. She didn't care if he hadn't received enough love from his mother or if he was bullied as a child. That didn't give him the right to treat her worse than an animal.

"This isn't right." He mimicked her, his lip curled with disgust. "And so what? Is there really anything about your pitiful life that is right? All that money and what have you done with it? Nothing. Nothing but party and make sure everyone knows your name. The beautiful Ange Matthews."

"That's not—"

His hand moved at lightning speed, and he slapped her. Hard. "Don't you call me a liar."

She bit her bottom lip to keep the tears from falling. He didn't like it when she cried. It made him angry. And that wasn't good. "I didn't mean it like that. But I really do give money to charities. All the time."

"I give money to charities." He mimicked her with a falsetto voice. "And that's supposed to justify your pitiful existence. Because you give a little money now

2

and then to some cause. Big deal. And no doubt, you make sure your picture is all over the news when you do. 'Look at me. I'm rich and I give money to the poor. I'm so good.' That's all you care about—having pictures of the beautiful Ange Matthews all over the place. Of course, you aren't all that beautiful right now, are you, Ange?"

Is that what this was about? Her money? Had he sent a ransom demand? "If you want my money, I'll give it to you. All of it. Please just let me go."

He stared at her as if thinking about her offer.

Hope surged. "Really. I'll give you my money. All of it. Every penny. Then you can go someplace where the police can't find you. There are countries that won't extradite you."

"Interesting idea but what would the beautiful Ange Matthews be without all her money? Do you think your celebrity friends would still want to hang around with you, Ange?" He shook his head. "But it might be nice to be rich for a change."

Please. Please. Take the money. If he wanted it, she would give it to him. *Every penny.* "We can go to the bank today."

He shrugged. "No, thanks. I love this country. And I'm a model citizen so I have no reason to leave."

The thought of freedom spurred her on. "Then stay here. I won't tell anyone about this. Please take my money, and let me go. How about a million dollars? I promise I won't tell anyone what you did. Ever." She sobbed now, unable to control it. "Please, I…I can't…let me go."

"This isn't my fault. It's yours." He pointed the knife at her then jabbed her in the arm with it. A spot of blood appeared. Beside all the other poke marks.

"It's not. It's not my fault. I—"

He slapped her face again, even harder. "I already warned you not to call me a liar. I said it's your fault. Tell me. Tell me that it's your fault." He held the knife close to her throat.

"Don't hurt me. It's…it's my fault."

"Of course it is. The beautiful Ange Matthews only cares about herself. No concern at all for those people you wanted me to leave behind. Not about how they would get home. How it would ruin their special evening. So very selfish of you." His finger pointed at her as if he was a school teacher giving her a lecture. "Your fault, not mine."

"I already told you I was sorry. You're right. I shouldn't have done that. It was selfish. And mean. But…but…I was upset. I'm so sorry. I promise I won't ever do it again. Please let me go." They'd had this same conversation countless times. And the results were always the same, but she couldn't stop herself from trying. One of these times it might work. He might take pity on her and free her.

"You're right about that because you'll not ever have a chance to do it again. Or anything else again, for that matter." His hand brushed her cheek and moved down. His fingers tightened around her throat. "But you know what? Even if I gave you a second chance, you'd probably do it again. That's just the kind of person you are. Selfish."

"I wouldn't. I'm not. I've changed. I promise."

His fingers squeezed until she couldn't breathe.

"I hate selfish people. Who knows, maybe you would change." His fingers relaxed, she gasped in air. "But it doesn't matter whether you changed or not since you'll never have the chance to prove it. You don't really think I could let you go, do you? After all, I am a model citizen. Can't let my reputation get tarnished. It wouldn't be good for business."

She stared at this monster. He seemed so normal, dressed in his work clothes with that stupid hat. To look at him, no one would know he was evil. Wouldn't know he had her trapped in his basement—or at least that's where she thought she was.

"Guess what? Nobody even cares that you're gone. Nothing's been on the news or the papers or even your precious social media. That just proves how worthless your life is."

"That's...that's not true." Everybody loved her. She had tons of friends. She was the life of the party. Actually, she was the party.

"Oh, isn't it? Then why haven't I heard a thing about the fact that the famous Ange Matthews is missing? Not one little peep on TV. I'll tell you why. Because nobody cares about you or your pitiful life. Only me. So you really should be nicer to me." He walked closer and put a hand on her shoulder as if comforting her.

Right! She jerked away from him.

His vicious slap stung once again. "I said be nice to me. Don't worry. I know it's been a difficult few weeks for you, but it won't last much longer."

"What does that mean?"

"What does that mean?" More mimicry, and then he smiled. "It means just what you think. You're not as much fun as I thought you'd be. I'm getting tired of this game with you. You're really quite boring, to tell the truth. All you do is whine and complain." He checked his watch and tipped his hat at her. "Gotta go. Duty calls." At the door he turned back. "Maybe tonight will be the night I end your suffering. Would you like that? Want me to end our little game, Ange?" He closed door and left. He'd left the light on this time.

Usually, he kept her in the darkness. She hated the dark now. She couldn't see him coming toward her. Couldn't ready herself for the next stab with the knife, or sometimes the whack of a hammer. Her body was one big bruise.

He hadn't done anything to her sexually. Which seemed odd to her. But every time he came back she thought this might be the day when that fear would become a reality as well.

It means what you think it means.

He had decided to kill her. She'd known that would happen sooner or later. Tonight might be the night. Unless she figured a way out. There had to be a way to escape from this mad man. She stared around at the tiny room that was her prison. If she could get untied then she might be able to get away. But it was almost impossible to even move.

There was no way to escape.

She would die here—and it really was her own fault.

2

The short slightly plump woman walked up to Nate Goodman's desk. "I need to talk to a co...policeman."

He smiled at her blunder. Some thought the word "cop" was an insult, but he wasn't one of them. He motioned for her to sit in a chair in front of his desk. "Then it's your lucky day because I happen to be one. What can I do for you, Miss…"

"I'm Keren Strong. K-E-R-E-N." She gave an embarrassed chuckle. "Sorry, force of habit. That's how I always introduce myself. I don't suppose you need to know how to spell by name."

"Not a problem, K-E-R-E-N." A little humor went a long way in putting people at ease. And this woman was anxious. "What can I do for you?"

She leaned forward in the chair, her fingers drumming on his desk. "I think my cousin's been kidnapped. I can't find her. Anywhere. She's simply disappeared, and I'm very worried about her."

Kidnapping wasn't a usual part of Nate's duties on the Mount Pleasant Police Department, population 17, 000, give or take a few hundred. He stared. "Excuse me?"

"I said I think my cousin's been kidnapped. Her name is Ange Matthews. I'm sure you've heard of her, right? Everybody has."

If anyone in Mt. Pleasant was to be kidnapped, it

would be Ange Matthews, their most famous and wealthy resident.

This woman didn't look as if she traveled in the same social circles as her glamorous, celebrity cousin. She was pretty but wore no makeup and her brown hair was a curly mess. A simple T-shirt with blue jeans completed her look.

"Really? What makes you think that?" He motioned to his boss and ex-fiancé, Leslie, the Chief of Police, to come over. "I think you better hear this. Go ahead; tell her what you told me."

"I think my cousin was kidnapped. Her name is Ange Matthews."

Leslie's eyes narrowed. "Why do you think she's been kidnapped?"

Keren clasped her hands together. "We were supposed to have lunch a week or so ago on Saturday, but she didn't show up. I haven't been able to get hold of her since then. Something's definitely wrong."

"And you say this is Ange Matthews?" Leslie asked.

"Yes, I'm sure you know she's very rich. Someone probably kidnapped her for her money. You've got to help her. I'm sure she's in trouble."

"How do you know she needs help? Has there been a ransom demand?" Leslie asked. "When was she kidnapped?"

"I don't really know if she was kidnapped, but something's wrong. I just…if not, why isn't she answering her phone?" She looked at Nate as if wanting him to step into the conversation. "Ange loves her phone, you know. She always has it with her. And even my husband is worried. He told me to come talk with you today."

"So you haven't received a ransom demand? Or any other type of communication that would indicate she's been kidnapped? That she's being held against her will?" Leslie asked as she sat down facing Keren.

"No but—"

"Then that probably means she's not been kidnapped. With her kind of money that would have been the first thing to happen. I'm sure she's fine." Leslie smiled at Keren. "I don't think it's a good idea to say she's been kidnapped when you have no such proof."

"Maybe there was a ransom but just not to me. How would I know? I'm only her cousin, and I'm sure not rich. The money's from her mother's side of the family. I'm from her father's side."

"Well, I'm sure if someone, anyone, had received a ransom demand, we would have been contacted about it." Leslie's tone told Nate she was no longer interested. "Besides, isn't she sort of known for traveling here and there all the time? She goes to New York and LA and other hot spots."

"Well, yes, but I can always get hold of her. But I can't this time. She's not answering her phone. And she always answers her phone. For me."

Leslie sighed. "Are the two of you close?"

"We see each other now and then. And we talk on the phone at least a few times a month. We were getting together for lunch a few Saturdays ago, and she never showed up. It was my birthday, so I don't think she'd just skip out without contacting me."

Nate hid his smile, understanding the situation a little bit better. Her rich, famous cousin had forgotten her birthday.

Leslie gave him a glance and a smirk. She was

probably thinking the same thing. Leslie looked back at the cousin. "Has she ever just left before? Without telling you."

"Well, sure, but—"

"So it is plausible she just left and isn't returning your calls. Because she's busy."

Leslie didn't have an ounce of concern for Ange Matthews or Keren, the cousin. Compassion was not her strong suit. That didn't surprise him.

Ange had probably thoughtlessly gone off somewhere, involved in her own pursuits, and had forgotten her cousin's birthday. The wealthy often had an entitlement personality, forgetting mere mortals who had to work for a living. He chided himself for making such a judgment. He didn't know her.

Keren's face was splotched with frustration. "Sure, it's plausible, but—"

"Then there's no case. We can't really help you." Leslie stood, dismissing the woman. "But be sure to contact us if you do get a ransom demand. Or have some real proof that she's missing." She walked away.

The woman looked at Nate. "I would have thought she'd be a little more concerned about Ange. Considering how rich and famous she is. And she does live in your town. I thought this was a friendly place."

"I'm sure she's concerned." He tried to be diplomatic. "But she's a busy woman. And I believe the Matthews Estate isn't actually within the city limits."

"Still. She wasn't very nice about it. And how busy could she really be? In this tiny town. It's not like it's Cleveland where there's real crime."

He couldn't disagree with her assessment about the town or Leslie so he said nothing.

"If she doesn't live right in town, does that mean it's not in your jurisdiction? Should I go someplace else?" She looked at him, obviously still wanting him to do something.

Nate thought about that for a moment. "Actually, I think this is the right place. It seems I remember something about the town expanding their city limits out past her house. Have you gone to her house?"

She nodded. "She wasn't there. Called her fiancé. He hadn't talked to her either."

"Didn't I read somewhere that she broke up with him?"

"Yea, I read that, too, but he didn't mention it when I called him. So I don't know if it really happened that way or that's just people blowing up an argument into more than it really was."

That was interesting. Keren had Ange's fiancé's phone number. So perhaps, her relationship was closer than he'd first thought. "Was he worried about her?"

"Not really. You know who he is, right? He's a Cleveland Browns player, and they're in training camp right now so he's been really busy. He probably hasn't had time to worry about her being gone."

"See, there you have it. I'm sure she's fine. If her fiancé isn't concerned, then there's probably nothing to worry about."

"Then why won't she return my calls? It doesn't make sense."

"Well maybe the two of them did break up. And that's probably why she hasn't wanted to talk to anyone. She's nursing a broken heart."

Her cousin laughed. "Nursing a broken heart? That doesn't sound like Ange at all. It's not her first broken engagement. She loves to get engaged, but marriage is a different story. I think she can't believe anyone wants to marry her unless it's for her money. Besides, it was my birthday. She wouldn't just blow me off like that."

Ange Matthews probably would do just that. Even though he'd never met her, her reputation was well-known. And it wasn't exactly a good one. "Look, I'll check into it a little, and if I find anything suspicious, I'll let you know. OK?"

She stood. "Thanks. Do you want my phone number?"

"Sure. And while you're at it, the fiancé's number as well. Hold on a minute." He walked over to a file cabinet and came back with a paper. "We might as well make this official. Fill this out and on the backside give me any information that might be helpful. Names and numbers of friends, including the fiancé. I don't know if you have access to any of her credit cards or such but that would be helpful as well."

"Oh, I don't have access to that at all. Like I said, I come from the other side of her family. Not the rich side."

What might that be like—having a very rich cousin who was also glamorous and famous? Keren obviously didn't have any of those things herself. Could this woman have led to her cousin disappearing? *Stop it. Not everyone is a suspect. You don't even know if the woman's really in trouble.*

After Keren left, he pulled his keyboard closer. He had an obligation to help. Ange Matthews deserved the same consideration as any one of the other citizens of Mt. Pleasant. It couldn't hurt to spend a few minutes checking out the situation.

Famous and rich. That probably added up to lots

of technology and social media. After twenty minutes at the keyboard, Nate had a good idea of Ange's life before she disappeared.

And he wasn't so sure Ange Matthew's cousin wasn't right.

Ange hadn't been on her public social media for more than a week. Before that, her posts were consistent. Since the Friday before she was to have lunch with Keren. Before that she was everywhere, the woman loved her social media. Her name was on all the major sites along with lots of news stories. She posted about anything and everything. And her followers seemed to love it. He didn't get why anyone would care what Ange Matthews had for breakfast, but they seemed to.

He stared out the window, his gaze focused on the bank. Did Ange Matthews use the town's only bank? Less than a minute later, he walked into that financial institution.

"Hey, Nate." Clint Smith gave him a wave from where he stood talking with one of the tellers.

"Just the man I'm looking for. Can we talk in your office?" Clint was the bank manager—or whatever his title was these days. It seemed to change from time to time, depending on what big bank had purchased it that week.

"Sure. Is there a problem?'

"Not a problem. I just have a question." He answered as they walked into the office.

Clint shut the door and motioned for him to sit.

Nate shook his head. "This won't take much time. I was wondering if Ange Matthews uses this bank."

Clint's eyes widened. "It's probably not legal for me to give you the answer to that question."

"Yeah, I sort of thought that's what you might say. But let me ask you this hypothetically."

Clint arched an orange-red brow. "Hypothetically?"

"I'm not just asking out of curiosity, you know."

"Then why are you asking?"

"Her cousin's worried about her. I'm sure it's nothing, but I figured one of the ways I could establish that it was, indeed, nothing was to see if her credit card transactions have been normal for the past week or so. So does she bank here?"

"I can't tell you that, but I can tell you I have met her on more than one occasion. If that helps." Clint walked around the desk and sat down at his computer. He looked up at Nate. "The last week or so? Hypothetically, of course."

"Of course."

A moment later Clint looked up with a worried expression. "Hypothetically speaking, it would be most unusual for someone like her to have no transactions for the past nine days."

"No transactions as in zero?"

Clint nodded. "What's going on, Nate?"

"I'm not at liberty to say. I was really hoping you'd tell me she went on a trip to some exotic location to nurse a broken heart, and she's there spending lots of her money."

"Well, I'm also sure our hypothetical person would have credit cards from other banks. That said, that someone likes our card. A lot."

"Can you access the info for me? About other cards?"

"Sorry. I can't do that even hypothetically."

"That's OK. I think I got what I needed. If you hear

from her or her cards are accessed, let me know."

"Hypothetically."

"Of course."

Nate walked across the street. It didn't appear as if Ange Matthews had gone on a last-minute trip somewhere. The last time she'd been on social media was the night she'd broken up with her fiancé. He needed to talk to the man.

He went to Leslie's office and knocked even though the door was open.

She motioned him in.

"There might be something to the cousin's concern about Ange Matthews."

"Really?" She arched a brow. "Why do you think that?"

"She hasn't been on social media or had a credit card charge since the night she broke up with her fiancé nine days ago. The Friday night before she was to have lunch with her cousin."

"Credit card? You have no right to access that info."

"I didn't. I just asked hypothetically. And got answered hypothetically."

She rolled her eyes. "Spare me the small-town bonding. You just said she broke up with her fiancé. She's probably off nursing a broken heart."

"Or maybe he wasn't happy that she broke it off with him in such a public way. Nobody likes to be humiliated. Didn't you see the news?"

"The football player, right?"

"Right."

She flipped a pencil back and forth. "Let it go, Nate. Ange Matthews is just off on another one of her trips somewhere. Everyone knows how she is. She's a spoiled brat who comes and goes as she pleases, without considering her cousin's feelings or her birthday."

"Then why hasn't she used her credit card or been on social media?"

"How would I know?"

"People don't just disappear without a reason. I think we have an obligation to at least check out the situation."

"Not true. It happens all the time, and you know it."

"She hasn't posted anything on her social media in more than a week. Before that, she was all over it. Dozens of times every day."

Leslie rolled her eyes. "You're just trying to figure out a way to meet the beautiful, rich girl now that you're an eligible bachelor again."

"You say that as if it's what I wanted. Remember, you're the one who broke it off and gave me back the ring. Because you have other things you want to do before you settle down. And this wasn't the place you wanted to settle down in anyway. Remember?"

Ignoring his words, she tapped her manicured nails on her desktop. "There's no case here, Nate."

"Her cousin thinks differently. And she drove all the way down here looking for her. That says something, doesn't it?"

"I'm sure it's not the first time Ange has been rude to her. Even the cousin admitted that she takes off on unscheduled jaunts without telling her."

"You're probably right, but I'm still going to look into it a little further."

"No, you're not. I said there's no case. And I'm still your boss."

"For the next few weeks anyway." He met her gaze and then leaned closer. "What if I'm right and you're wrong? What if Ange Matthews really is missing and you did nothing about it? It might mess up your meteoric rise at the FBI if they find out you didn't follow up on a citizen's complaint about her missing cousin."

Leslie's eyes narrowed. "Fine. You want to waste your time, waste it. What do I care?"

"Leslie, I really don't understand where this animosity's coming from. You broke up with me, not the other way around. I didn't stand in your way when the FBI accepted your application."

"For a cop, you are clueless." She held up her hands in surrender. "Go do what you want. I have an appointment." She made a grand exit from her office.

The others in the squad room pretended not to notice their argument.

He had a feeling she regretted giving back his ring, but it was a done deal. And he had no plans to undo the deal. She may have been the one to make the decision, but it was the right decision. For both of them. He was more than happy living here in his hometown. Not her—she'd never be happy living here permanently. Mount Pleasant was only a stepping stone to other places—more glamorous places with a lot more action. Leslie was also wrong about his interest in Ange Matthews. Beautiful and rich was way too high maintenance for his taste. Nate liked simple.

He'd learned that lesson from Leslie.

Well, there were two ways to work a case. Old-fashioned footwork or new-fashioned computer work. He'd found out what he could on the computer. Now, it was time for old-fashioned police work. There were things that could only be learned by talking to people. Technology helped, but people solved crimes.

First a trip to the Brown's training facility in Berea and then to the last place she'd been seen: Cleveland. He hated big cities.

3

Her death would be her own fault. She should have known better. One minute she'd stepped up to a limo, and the next she was here. He'd asked her to call him Luther, and that was all she remembered until she woke up trapped in this basement. He was drugging her. Day and night morphed into each other with large chunks of time missing in between. She wasn't quite sure low long she'd been here, but it was more than enough for someone to report the fact that she was missing.

Surely someone had contacted the police by now. Unless Luther was right? Maybe nobody cared enough to notice she was gone. No, she had to believe they were looking for her right this minute. Weren't they? Panic slammed back into her as strong as Luther's slap. She took a deep breath, her eyes fluttering. *Keep me sane, God, in this insane place.*

Zarlengo probably wouldn't notice she was missing, not after what she did to him.

If only she could go back to that night. Her mind went back in time to the restaurant. Reliving it probably wasn't the healthiest choice but she couldn't help herself. It had been her last few minutes of freedom.

She'd talked Zarlengo into taking her to a five-star restaurant where most people had to wait for months to get a reservation, but all they'd done that evening was walk in and ask for a table. The owner had been more than happy to have the two of them as guests.

The handsome football player and his beautiful fiancé.

Her lip quivered as she looked down at the dirty T-shirt she wore. There wasn't anything beautiful about her any more.

It had been between the appetizer and the soup when she'd chosen to exact revenge on her unfaithful fiancé. He'd humiliated her in public, and now, it was her turn to do the same to him. Turnabout was fair play.

Handsome, rich, and famous didn't add up to good husband material—or even make for a good boyfriend. Time and time again, she'd forgiven him for his indiscretions as he promised her it wouldn't happen again. But it always did.

She'd jumped up from the table with a flourish. When she'd been sure that all eyes were on them, she'd slid the ring off her finger. She'd tossed her blonde curls back and said, "Just because you're the Cleveland quarterback doesn't mean you can treat me like this. I won't tolerate it."

His handsome face turned splotchy red. Good. "Sit down, Ange," he whispered through clenched teeth. "Don't cause a scene. I said I was sor—"

"I don't want to hear any more of your excuses or your apologies. We're done." She flung the ring at him. Giving her blonde hair another angry toss, she weaved her way among the tables.

The other customers watched her departure, some surreptitiously, others were more blatant. Camera phones pointed her way. There must have been a lot of action on social media that night.

And that was exactly what she'd intended. Zarlengo's flings were well-hidden from his adoring fans. Everyone assumed he was a fine, upstanding young man. He deserved to be exposed for the liar he was.

And that was exactly what she'd done.

Once outside, she'd wiped away sincere tears as her hopes and dreams had crashed. At one point, she'd really believed Zarlengo was the one.

She'd hurried up to the doorman. "I need you to call me a cab. And tell them to hurry. Please. I need to get out of here."

The doorman pulled out his cell phone.

But she'd spied a limo parked across the street. Heading for it, she'd called back. "Never mind. I just found my own ride." She'd knocked on the window and forced her most charming smile.

The driver's window slid down.

"I need a ride."

He smiled, his bright blue eyes crinkling at the corners. "Sorry, ma'am. I'm waiting for some other customers. Want me to—"

"Oh, come on. I'll pay you double what they're paying. I need to get out of here. Now." She gave him a sweet smile with just a bit of flirt. "Please."

"You don't even know what they're paying me."

Giving him another sunny smile, she shrugged. "Doesn't matter. I'll pay it. Actually, I'll pay you a thousand dollars. How does that sound? And you can probably be back before your other customers even know you're gone. I only want to go to a downtown hotel. Won't take but a few minutes. You'll be back before they get finished eating. They probably won't even know you left."

"Hey, I know you."

She leaned down, allowing her silky white blouse to droop an extra inch or so, knowing it looked good against her tan. "That's right, I'm Ange Matthews. Now will you take me to the hotel?"

He tore his gaze from her chest. "Let me see the money."

It was a rare day when someone told her no. "We can stop at an ATM along the way. How's that sound?"

His door opened and he jumped out with a smile.

Good, this was more like the service she was accustomed to.

"Let me get that door for you, Ms. Matthews." He took hold of her arm and moved closer. Something jabbed her in the arm.

"Ouch. What was that?"

She'd tried to pull her arm away, but he'd held on tight. Then he smiled.

"Nothing for you to worry about, Ange."

Her head began to spin as her eyes lost focus. Now there was two of him. She tried to blink away the extra man. He stayed. "Wh...at...happened? What did...you do?"

"I told you not to worry about it, Ange."

With a little push, she tumbled into the limo. Something...wrong. She tried to sit up but her muscles didn't seem to be working. Not...good. "I... I...changed...my mind. Let me out."

The door slammed shut. The whole world was spinning. It looked so far away, but Ange reached for the latch. She needed to get out of here. The lock clicked.

"Let...me..." Too hard to think. Too tired. Her eyes closed. And when she opened them again, she was in this room. Trapped by a monster.

Each day she was in this prison made it more likely that she would never get out. Never see the sky again or breathe fresh air. Never…tears seeped out as her list continued. She twisted her body. Ignoring the pain, she closed her eyes as the ropes cut into her already raw wrists and ankles. And as always, she could barely move.

If she escaped it wouldn't be through her brute strength.

Luther kept talking about how pretty girls thought they were so much better than everyone else. Someone pretty must have hurt him so much that he'd become a monster.

She assessed her situation. She had no sheets or coverings of any sort, just the dirty t-shirt. He'd taken her clothes along with her freedom and dignity. If beauty or strength wouldn't help, that left brains. Her Daddy had said she was as smart as she was pretty. There had to be a way out of this mess.

"Please God. Help me." The spoken words showed how truly desperate she'd become.

God wouldn't help her, and she didn't have any right to expect Him to. It had been a long time since she'd prayed or been to church. She'd been a believer, once.

But now…not since her parents' funeral.

Her parents had been strong believers. God was a part of their home and their everyday life. Her parents believed in moral absolutes, in right and wrong, in good and bad, and in godliness and evil.

That had been a long time ago.

Ange had drifted away from God. Perhaps, if she hadn't drifted so much, she might not be trapped here.

Her parents had told her time and time again that God would always be there, waiting for her. What was that verse? Something about drawing near to God and he would draw near to her. Was it true? She called out. "God, are you there? Can you hear me? Do you still love me?" She closed her eyes, waiting for a miracle. Then she opened her eyes and stared at the rope around her wrists.

God didn't come down and untie them.

"Yeah, that's what I thought." She spoke out loud. "I don't blame you, God. I don't really like me any more either. So why should you?"

Luther was right about one thing. She really hadn't done much with her life in spite of the opportunities she'd been blessed with. Mama and Daddy would be disappointed in her. They believed in hard work and giving back. She'd never worked a day in her life. Never did anything useful. Nothing for her to be proud of. All she'd ever focused on was how often she'd made the TV reports or magazines. How many friends and followers she had.

The really important things in life—not!

"I'm so sorry." She wasn't sure if she was talking to her parents or to God.

Staring at the stained mattress, she was pretty sure she wasn't the first person Luther had tied up to it. Or hurt or tortured on it. He needed to be stopped. It wasn't right for anyone to be treated this way.

Anger stirred inside her.

If he killed her, he'd find another woman to do this to. And then another and another. How many times—how many women before he got caught? She wouldn't let him get away with this. She glared at the door of her tiny prison. "I'll be the last one you hurt!"

4

Nate showed Ange Matthews's picture to the doorman at the restaurant. And yes, somewhere between leaving Mt. Pleasant, talking with Zarlengo, the quarterback, and driving here, he'd decided Ange Matthews was, indeed, missing. "What do you think? Does she look familiar?"

"Sure. It's Ange Matthews. Everyone knows her. She comes here quite often. We're her favorite restaurant. She was dating that Browns' player. I think he's the quarterback. Not sure, I don't follow sports all that much. Anyway, yes, I know her."

"When was the last time you saw her?"

He shrugged. "I don't know. A week or two ago."

"You can do better than that. A little more specific."

"Not really. A lot of people come in and out of here. After a while they all sort of morph into one big crowd, even the famous ones. But you can check with reservations, I'm sure they'll know."

"I'll do that in a minute, but what can you tell me about the last time you saw her?"

"Look, it's not my place to gossip. I get paid to hold the door open for people and to help them find a cab if they need it. Not gossip. And not make judgments about what they do or how they act."

Interesting. What had he seen Ange Matthews do that he didn't like? "I get that, but it's not gossip. I already told you I'm a police officer." He pulled out his badge. Nate had not worn his uniform. Mount Pleasant was too small to have a detective, but that didn't mean they didn't need one now and then. So he'd traded in his uniform for a suit.

The doorman stared at his badge and then back up at Nate. "Yeah, but not a Cleveland one."

"Really? That makes a difference?" He toughened up the tone of his voice, something he didn't do often. "I'm just trying to find her. To make sure she's all right. She might be in trouble, you know. Was she alone when she left? Did you get her a cab? I need to know what you know."

The doorman gave him a skeptical look. "Is she really missing?"

"According to her family she is. I'm not some paparazzi looking for her." He held up the badge again. "I work for Mt. Pleasant Police Department where she lives. Her cousin filed a missing person's report. I'm just here doing my job so…"

"That's too bad. She seems nice enough. She comes in regularly." He sighed, clearly not happy about being questioned.

"What happened the last time you saw her? Anything you tell me could be important."

"She didn't come in alone, but she left alone. She was clearly upset when she left. I found out later she caused a big scene inside the restaurant, but I didn't actually see that. If you can't find her, maybe you should talk to the boyfriend. That Cleveland Brown player."

"Already did. Says he hasn't talked to her since the night in the restaurant. Giving her time to cool off. And he's been at training camp since then. So he has a great alibi." Zarlengo thought she'd taken off on one of her trips. "So what happened when she came out?"

"I started to call a cab for her, but then she saw a limo waiting over there." He motioned with his head. "And told me to forget about the cab. So I did."

"Did she leave in the limo?"

He nodded, his expression not happy. "Last I saw, she got into the limo. Not her limo, but someone else's. Another couple came out and was quite agitated that their limo had disappeared. Of course, I didn't tell them about Ange absconding with it. I did call them a cab. Now that's all I know."

"What was the name of the limo company?"

"I have no idea."

"What was the name of the other couple?"

"I have no idea. Check with—"

"Reservations."

"Now you've got the idea."

Five minutes later, Nate was back in his car with a copy of the reservations from that night. Names and phone numbers. He struck out on the first three calls. He pressed in the fourth number and waited.

"Hello." A woman answered.

"This is Nate Goodman. I'm a police officer from Mount Pleasant."

"Never heard of it."

"It's a small town south of Cleveland in Wayne County. Is this Lisa McDonald?"

"Is there a problem? Did I do something wrong?"

"Not at all. I'm just checking on something. I heard you had some trouble with a limo a week or so ago when you were at a restaurant."

"Yes, but it was all a big mix up. He gave us our money back and a free limo ride for another time. So no big deal."

"What was the mix up?"

A slight pause. "Why are you interested? We didn't do anything wrong."

"Of course not. I'm just doing some follow up on a case. It doesn't have anything to do with you, I promise. I really only need the name of the limo company."

"Are you sure?"

"Absolutely but I have to admit my curiosity is getting the better of me. So I was kind of wondering what actually happened."

"Apparently, the limo driver didn't realize we wanted him to wait for us. So he left after he dropped us off. He thought we were just a drop-off with no return trip. I was a bit irritated at the time, but hey, a free limo ride. Can't beat that for a little inconvenience."

"That's for sure." So the limo driver had lied to Lisa McDonald. But that didn't prove anything. The driver was probably just trying to keep out of trouble with his own boss.

"As I said, no big deal. It's not the first time my husband messed up on something like that. He's hopeless when it comes to details. I'll not even tell you what happened the last time he booked our vacation flights. Not that you care, but from now on, I'll be making the reservations."

"And what's the limo company?"

"Not a limo company, my husband likes to support small businesses whenever he can. It's a single driver. An independent driver, I guess you'd call him."

"Got his name and number?"

Another pause. "Why? Is he in trouble? Did he do

something wrong?"

"Not that I know of. Is there a problem with giving his information to me?"

"Not that I know of." She laughed. "Hold on, I'll see if I can find his card. I'm sure I've got it somewhere." A moment later, she was back. "His name is Luther Marks."

Nate's fingers flew across the keyboard of the in-car computer as he typed in the driver's name. Seconds later the screen flashed the results.

Old-fashioned footwork. He'd never have found out about the limo driver if he hadn't talked to the doorman in person. On a hunch, he called the police department in Luther Marks' jurisdiction and previous home, a town in West Virginia.

After hanging up, his blood ran cold.

~*~

He was home.

His footsteps clunked above her head. She assumed she was in the basement, but she really had no idea. She could be in a barn or an abandoned warehouse. This was the only room she'd been in since she'd woken up. There were no windows to tell her whether it was night or day. She stared at the gray concrete walls.

What kind of a limo driver kept a syringe with knockout drugs on him? One who tied women up and then tortured them. And then killed them. The kind of man one read about in the news or saw in horror movies. The kind of man no one ever really believed they'd meet.

Tears leaked as she contemplated the situation.

There had to have been other victims. The mattress told that story. The story of pain and torture...and death, she was sure of it. Since none of them had come forward and pointed an accusing finger at him.

That could only mean one thing.

He had to be a serial killer, not just a sadistic kidnapper. He was pure evil. The look of pure bliss...and excitement on his face when he walked toward her was disgusting—and evil.

No matter what she'd done she didn't deserve to be treated like this. Did Zarlengo even realize she was missing? Did he care? Probably not. Too busy with his own life to notice.

The night before the restaurant, he'd been filmed at a downtown nightclub with, not one, but two women. It didn't take a genius to figure out how he'd spent the rest of his evening. It probably didn't bother Zarlengo all that much that she'd given back his ring, but his image was important to him. One of the reasons she'd decided to end it publicly as well.

Surely, he wasn't behind this, hiring someone to do his dirty work. He wouldn't be all that upset about their relationship being over. He'd just move on to his next woman. It was so clear now that he had no intention of being faithful to her. Why she'd even accepted the engagement ring was a mystery.

Ange had just wanted to get as far away from him as she could that night. She'd certainly accomplished that. If she hadn't decided to humiliate Zarlengo, she wouldn't be here. She should have stayed home that night and read a book.

So...Luther was right again. Her fault. No one to

blame but herself.

Something crashed above.

Uneasiness filled her, but there was little she could do. Ange went back to her thoughts. She wouldn't have to worry about her choices in men anymore.

It wasn't as if she'd ever have the opportunity to marry anyone—ever. Or even smell fresh air again. Perhaps Luther would bring her something to eat today. Her stomach hurt. The food probably had drugs in it. But that was a price she'd gladly pay. And sleeping made the time go faster.

This was what her life had become. Hoping that a madman would give her drugged food. She squeezed her eyes shut. *Don't think about that. Stay focused on getting out of here.*

But all the hours she'd been in this filthy bed had given her time to assess her life. She had a few charities that she supported. But her life was about her. Shopping. Getting on TV. Dating famous men. Living the beautiful life. Wanting other people to envy her.

If she got out of here, that would change. She wasn't sure what she'd do, but her life would be different. That was a promise. She'd promised this would be the day she escaped too, and yet she was still here. But she had a plan now.

It might even work.

The door opened. "How was your day, sweetheart?" His chuckle echoed against the cement block walls.

His laugh sent a chill up her spine and straight to her heart. She closed her eyes. *Please, God, give me the strength I need.* Opening her eyes, she forced a smile with as much sweetness as she could muster. "How was your day, Luther?"

"As if you care."

Give me the right words. "Of course, I care. I know it's not easy dealing with all the people you do, and how they're only concerned about themselves. And their needs. Nobody worries about your needs."

"So I'm supposed to believe this change of heart in you?" His mocking tone told her he wasn't buying her new attitude. He walked over to the table—his back to her. To his tools.

How she wished she could grab one and hurt him the way he'd hurt her. She shuddered as he touched one and then another. He was deciding what to do to her tonight. She couldn't take another night of his torture.

Don't think about the bad. Just be nice. "Believe what you want, but it's true. As you said this morning, you're the only one here to take care of me so, of course, I care about you. If something happened to you, what would become of me tied up down here?"

He turned and looked at her, a spark of interest in his gaze. "It's about time you figured that out. That's exactly what I've been telling you. But, of course, I know you just want something from me. That's why you're pretending to be nice all of a sudden."

"I do want something from you. I want you to let me up so I can..." Can what? Her mind searched for something to say. "So I can cook dinner for you. Wouldn't you like that? I know I always love it when someone cooks dinner for me."

"I'm supposed to believe you want to cook me dinner." He laughed. "I'm almost tempted to agree. Just to see what happens. A rich girl like you probably never cooked a day in her life."

Hopefully, he liked scrambled eggs or spaghetti.

That was the limit of her repertoire. She forced her voice to sound cheerful, almost flirty. "Well, let me up and find out. Let me take care of you tonight."

It seemed like forever that he stared at her. He had to trust her.

Please, God.

He walked closer and then leaned down. "I'm tempted, but I'm not that stupid."

Hope seeped out of her.

"You want me to let you up so you can figure out a way to escape. And all those weapons you'd have access to in a kitchen. Knives. Fire. Hot water. So sorry I'm not that stupid." He paused. "You can't escape from me. There's no reason to try."

She had to try. Not just for her, but to protect his next victim. "I don't think you're stupid at all, Luther. It's quite obvious you're a very intelligent man. How else could you pull this off?" She didn't know any man that wasn't susceptible to a little ego-stroking.

"What makes you say that?" He gave a slight smile as if her flattery had worked.

"I don't think I'm the first person you've kept here. And you've managed not to get caught, so I'd say you're pretty smart. I could promise not to try to escape, but you'd know that was a lie. Instead, why not take a chance and see if I can cook or not? I'm getting a little bored. Let's change up the game a bit. You do like games, right, Luther?"

He turned back to his table and picked up something. When he turned back, Ange's heart rate spiked even as any courage she'd built up failed her. In one hand was a gun; in the other a knife—a huge knife. As he moved closer to her, evil emanated from him. He planned to kill her. Right now. This was it. She squeezed her eyes shut, not wanting to see the knife come at her.

"Open your eyes, Ange." His tone told her not to disobey.

When she opened them, he smiled.

"I'd plan to kill you tonight. Like I said, you haven't been all that much fun. But you've upped the game a bit. So…" He brought the knife to her throat. "Let's have a little fun tonight."

The blade scraped against her skin. He pressed the point into her throat. In the next moment, the knife moved from her throat. He slashed through one of the ropes. She wanted to slap out at him with her free hand but didn't dare.

"So we'll play your game tonight. I'll let you cook for me. Right? That's what you wanted to do. Take care of me."

She nodded.

The knife slashed through the rope holding her other wrist.

"But if you even try to escape…" He held up the gun. "Game over."

"I understand." Sooner or later he'd kill her, so if she had the opportunity, she'd go for it. If not tonight, another time. Now that she'd talked him into letting her up once, maybe she could do it again. She'd accomplished her first step. He trusted her enough to let her up.

Daddy was right—she did have brains. "You can trust me."

"Yeah, right. But if you do anything I don't like, I'll simply shoot you. No warnings. No second chances. Got it?" He waved the gun as he moved down to the end of the bed and freed her legs.

After he freed her, she stayed still. Waiting. She knew the drill. No moving without permission.

Finally, he nodded. "You can get up."

She moved to a sitting position, her legs dangled off the edge. Slowly she slid off the bed until her feet touched the floor. She held on to the bed for support, waiting for her legs to steady.

"So, what were you thinking about cooking for me, Ange?"

5

Nate slowed as he drove past the mailbox for the third time. Big red letters spelled the name LUTHER MARKS. The rural stretch of road was sparsely populated, a few houses scattered far apart. If one needed privacy, especially the kind of privacy Luther Marks would want, this was a great place.

According to Luther Marks' records, he'd been arrested several times for domestic battery and assault. Even more interesting was the phone call to the police department of his last known address. Not in Ohio, but in his native West Virginia. According to the officer, Nate had spoken with, Luther Marks had been questioned in the disappearance of two women. No charges were ever filed in those cases since the bodies hadn't been found. The words had chilled Nate. Not wanting to waste valuable time, he hadn't taken the time to investigate all of Luther's past. He had more than enough proof, even if it wasn't enough for a judge to give him a warrant. Nate had a feeling there'd be other missing women in the other places Luther had lived. But that would have to wait until later.

Right now, Nate's only concern was Ange Matthews. He prayed it wasn't too late. Ange had been missing more than a week—more than enough time for…well more than enough time.

Luther had moved to Ohio and started his limo service. He hadn't had any serious run-ins with the law since living here. But that didn't mean he wasn't breaking the law now.

On yet another trip past, Nate stared down the long lane. If he drove down it, surely Luther would hear him coming. And if he heard Nate that would give him time to do any number of things. If Nate sneaked back and knocked on the door, the man would wonder how he'd gotten there in the first place.

Either way could endanger Ange Matthews—if she was in the house.

Nate stared through the trees at the rundown farm house. A stranded motorist would have to pick Luther's house if he was looking for a phone. Time for some role playing. He pulled off the road, thankful he'd driven his personal car. He stepped out of the vehicle, took off his suit jacket, walked to the trunk, and opened it. He pulled out his spare tire and leaned it against the car so it could be seen from the house. Taking the jack and the lug wrench out of its spot, Nate knelt down and pretended to jack up the car. Then he acted as if he was trying to remove the lug nuts. Not that he had any intention of doing that. He stood up and kicked the car tire as he debated whether to call the county sheriff's office. But what could he tell them that could even warrant backup? He had no real evidence, only a suspicion.

His only backup would have to be his gun.

He walked back to the driver's side of his car, untucking his shirt, and then slid the gun into the waistband of his pants. He didn't want a confrontation unless it was absolutely necessary. But Nate wanted the protection, just in case. And he uttered a quick prayer for God's protection, too. At the last minute, he called Leslie.

She picked up on the first ring. "Where are you?"

After explaining, he gave her the address. "There's no evidence to call in a warrant. But I thought someone should know where I was before I actually go to the house to talk to him."

"I don't like it, Nate." All the nonchalance of not believing there was even a case had vanished. Two missing women could do that. "I think you should wait until we get more evidence and can get a warrant."

And Ange Matthews could be dead by that time.

"I'll be fine. I'll call you as soon as I leave the house."

"No—"

"Yes. You said it was my case, so I'm doing what I think is best. For Ange Matthews. And besides if you were here, you'd do the same thing. I know it."

"Fine." Resignation rang in her voice. "Call me as soon as you leave there."

"Got it." After disconnecting, he opened the back of his phone and slid out the battery. Then he placed the battery in his pocket and the phone under his seat. His gaze fell on the small police-issued laptop. Leaning back in the car, he slid that under the passenger side, accepting the possibility that Luther might actually came out to help him.

As he walked down the lane, he eyed the house. In the dusk of the day, the large farm house looked even more foreboding—almost evil. After another quick prayer, he moved toward it. With every step he took, the sky darkened a bit more. A storm was coming. His breath turned ragged—from nerves and not from exertion. Pride was not one of his faults any longer. But he had plenty of other ones to worry about. He scanned the property in the dim light. There was a shed and a detached garage on the property. Further back sat a huge old barn.

Ange could be in any of those buildings, fighting for her life.

But there was no way to check it out at this point. The best he could do was talk with Luther and hope the man said something—anything—that would give Nate a chance at a warrant. Forcing his breathing to slow, he kept walking. It wouldn't do for Luther to see him nervous.

~*~

"Can I get cleaned up before I cook? I'm just so dirty." She gestured at the ragged t-shirt she wore.

They stood in Luther's kitchen.

It was cleaner than she'd expected. She fought the urge to look for a weapon of some sort. Instead, Ange kept her gaze on Luther, hoping he would relax. The gun frightened her, but if she saw a chance to get away, she would take it.

"I suppose." He escorted her upstairs to the bathroom and watched her every move.

When she finished, he grabbed her arm and walked her to the bedroom.

Her heart sank as she stared at the bed, but she would do what she had to do to survive. Anything to stay alive. Anything to get him to trust her so she had a chance of escaping.

He motioned with the gun for her to walk into the room. Once there, he let go of her arm, walked over to a dresser, and tossed her a clean T-shirt.

"Thanks." She said as she pulled the oversized shirt over her head. It was hard not to notice how thin she'd become in the past week and a half. She forced a smile. "OK, now I'm ready to cook. What's your favorite food?"

His eyes glittered with suspicion as he held up the gun. "Remember, there won't be any warnings. If you do anything I don't like, anything at all, it's over." He waved the gun around the room. "Got it?"

"I understand. I'll be good. I just want to cook something for you." She prayed that he might even let her eat a bite or two. By her calculations, she'd not eaten for the past two days. "What do you want me to cook?"

"I'll leave that up to you. Surprise me." He grabbed hold of her arm as they walked down the stairs.

She wanted to bolt to the front door, but she'd be shot in the back if she tried.

"I've got a couple of pork chops in the fridge."

Pork chops. Her mouth watered. "Got any vegetables? And rice. I do a mean stir-fry." Not exactly true, but she'd watched her cook do it several times. She thought she could manage it.

It wasn't likely there'd be any chance to escape tonight. This was about getting him to trust her—and not to kill her. If he trusted her, he might start giving her more freedom. More freedom would mean more opportunities. The escaping would come later. She hoped.

"I should have guessed a rich girl like you would want to cook up something fancy." He twisted her arm to emphasize his point. "But I probably have a few.

You can look in the fridge."

"If you prefer, I can just fry them. Whatever you—"

"Yeah, right. I'm sure—"

Someone knocked on the front door.

He froze mid-step.

Then he squeezed her arm so tight it brought tears to her eyes. She couldn't believe it. Someone was actually at the door. Someone who could help her?

"If you don't want to die right this moment, you'd better not make a sound." His arm snaked around her neck. His whisper was more like a serpent's hiss than a human voice. "Understand?"

"I understand." Her gaze focused on the door. Who was standing on the other side? Had God actually sent someone to help her? Had He answered her prayer?

With his nails still digging in to her flesh, he dragged her down the last few steps as he called, "Be there in a minute." He pressed the gun against her side as he held her close to him. The smell of fear rose from him.

Rather than being comforted that he was afraid, it terrified her. His fear could lead to her death. And for whoever was outside.

He didn't open the door but yelled out, "What do you want?"

"I got a flat tire. And my lug nuts won't come off. And wouldn't you know my cell phone's dead. Talk about bad luck. Anyway, I need to call road service to come out to help."

Luther's gaze never left her face as the man talked.

If only she had the courage to scream. Tell him to run, to call the police, but terror prevented her from doing anything. Not just for her, but for the stranger at the door.

If Luther pulled the trigger, would it kill her? It might be worth the risk. He had no intention of letting her live when he was done playing his games anyway. Maybe she should take the chance.

Luther was thinking about shooting her right that moment, if his glittering eyes and evil expression were any indication. If she even made a move or yelled for help, he'd kill her. And then he'd probably shoot the poor man on the other side of the door who'd picked the wrong house. It was one thing to risk her own life, but someone else's? She wouldn't do that. She forced her muscles to relax, hoping Luther would do the same.

"No need to do that." Luther suddenly yelled. "I'll get my tools and come out. It will just take me a minute to get them. I'll meet you at your car."

"Great. Thanks so much. Think I can get a drink of water? It was a long walk down that lane."

"I've got a bottle somewhere. I'll bring it out to you."

"I could really use it right now."

"Look, mister, you want me to help you or not?"

Ange wanted the man to go away before he got them both killed.

"No problem. Just bring it out when you come." His voice told her he was clueless as to the drama he was creating inside the house. Or how close he was to dying—or her dying.

"Be there in a minute." Even as Luther was saying the words, he started dragging her back toward the kitchen and the basement. "You better stay shut up if you know what's good for you. Got it?"

Tears filled her eyes as she looked back toward the door and windows. All covered. There was no way that man could see her. She'd had her chance to escape but hadn't found the courage to yell at the man to get help. But it wasn't too late. She could still yell. But if she did that, she'd be putting his life in danger, too.

If she had to die, she'd rather die knowing she'd not caused another person's death.

As they passed the refrigerator she looked at it longingly. Pork chops. There'd certainly be no food tonight. Luther would probably come back and kill her after he dealt with the man at the door. He'd probably kill him, too.

"Good girl. You're very lucky you didn't yell. I would have shot you dead." He glared at her. "I know you wanted to."

She shook her head. "I...just...want to cook dinner. That's all."

Luther opened the door to the basement and shoved her in. She fell on the landing.

"I'm locking the door, and you won't be able to get out. If you try, I'll kill you. So you just get down those steps and in that bed and wait for—"

Glass shattered in the living room, and then a loud thump sounded.

"Police!"

God had answered Ange's prayers. Hope stabbed through her so fast it made her breathless.

Luther's face paled and then turned bright red. He swirled away from her and ran toward the living room with the gun aimed toward the open doorway.

"He's got a gun," she screamed even as she moved toward the kitchen drawers to get a weapon.

"Get out of here!" the man yelled from the living

room. "Go. Run."

The kitchen door was right there, the way to freedom. But she couldn't just leave that man alone with Luther. Maybe he'd yelled, "police" because he'd seen something through the windows that made him realize she needed his help. If he was the police, he probably had a weapon. If not, they'd both be in trouble. It wouldn't be right to just run away and leave him alone.

Gunshots exploded in the next room.

No time to search for a knife. Her gaze fell on the stove. A frying pan. That would have to do. More gun shots rang out as she charged into the room with the frying pan held up high. With all the force she could muster, she raised the frying pan and whacked Luther in the back of the head.

He moaned and crumpled to the floor.

The floor was littered with glass. The blind hung halfway down. Apparently, the man had jumped through the window. Her would-be rescuer was on the floor with a gun in his hand. His shirt was covered in blood.

"You're shot!" she screamed at him as adrenaline pouring through her system.

He managed to stand. "I'm O—" His hand reached toward her as he swayed, and then he collapsed on the floor in front of her.

Horrified, she bent down and began shaking him. "Get up. Get up."

Luther grabbed her hair. "You should have run like he told you to, Ange. Now both of you are going to die."

She couldn't let Luther take her back to the basement. She reached out for the man, her fingers wrapped around his arm. As Luther pulled her hair, she slid away. Her hand scraped down the man's arm to his fingers. Her gaze fell on his gun. Her fingers curled around the weapon as Luther dragged at her.

She turned and squeezed the trigger, but nothing happened.

Luther still had her hair clutched in his hand. He lifted her up to him. "Too bad the gun was out of bullets. You'll pay for that." He slapped her.

Bright silvery stars clouded her vision as he grabbed for the gun, but she tossed it away.

He punched her in the face. More stars.

She moaned.

A moment later, he punched her in the stomach. When he loosened his grasp on her hair, she crumpled to the floor. She gasped for air, unable to take a breath.

Luther walked toward the other man, his gun aimed at the stranger, who was still unconscious.

She couldn't let the man die. Ignoring the pain, she moved to her knees, and then stood. It took every ounce of willpower to remain upright. "I'm outa here," she yelled and hobbled toward the kitchen, expecting a bullet in her back.

Luther cursed.

The bullet missed her as it smashed into the wall beside her.

She ran to the kitchen door and began to unbolt it. Had to get out. Before he killed her.

"Stop! One more move, and I'll shoot you."

At least he hadn't shot that man. She held up her hands in surrender and turned toward him. "Don't hurt me. Please. I'll do anything you want, Luther. Don't kill me."

Luther's pants leg was dark with blood. Maybe he

would bleed to death before he had time to kill her. She had to delay the inevitable as long as she could.

"I've had enough. I warned you." He advanced toward her. "Now it's time for you to die." The wound didn't seem to be slowing him down.

She cowered against the door. "Please don't. I'll do anything you want. Let's go play your games."

His hands went around her throat. "Forget about shooting you. I want to enjoy this." He squeezed tighter. His eyes shined with hatred.

She couldn't breathe. She flailed her arms, hitting at him.

He was too strong.

Her lungs longed for air. Stars clouded her vision and the darkness slipped closer.

"Let go of her, or I'll shoot. Now."

Luther twisted her into a neck hold and spun her in front of him. A tap of cold steel pressed against her temple as he put the gun to her head. She sucked in blessed air, too grateful for the lungful to think of the drama around her.

"You don't have any bullets."

"I reloaded." The man pointed the gun at Luther. "I said let go of her. Now." He advanced toward them.

"I don't care if that's true. It's not going to happen." Luther snarled as he tightened his arm around her neck. "Don't take another step, or I'll shoot her. Then it'll be your turn. Either way you both die. And I live."

The man stopped walking. His gaze met hers as if to say 'sorry.'

"You put that gun down on the floor. Nice and easy and then kick it toward me. Or I'll kill her. Now. I know I have more bullets. Want to take that risk?"

Luther's growl grated.

Her would-be rescuer seemed to run through the possibilities. But his hesitation would get him killed. She wasn't worth it. Tears streamed down her face. "Just kill him. Don't worry about me. He plans to kill us anyway."

Luther clicked the hammer on his gun, still pressed against her head.

"Don't shoot her." The man held his hands up in surrender. "I'm putting the gun down."

"No. No. Shoot him."

He placed the gun on the floor.

Now they would both die.

The gun moved from her head.

"Good choice," Luther said. "Are you really a cop?"

The man shook his head. "I saw you dragging her through the room. I couldn't just walk away. I thought I could help."

Could he really see through those blinds?

"Don't you lie to me, boy. What about your gun?"

"I keep it in the car for protection. I brought it with me because I didn't know who lived in this house. For all I knew it could be some crazy guy. Guess I was right about that."

The answer seemed to satisfy Luther. "OK. Both of you in the basement. I'll deal with the two of you later. I've got to get your car off the road before it attracts attention. Where's your keys?"

"In my pocket."

"Throw 'em to me, and your cell phone."

The man put a hand in his pocket and tossed the keys in their direction. "Don't have a cell phone. Remember that's why I'm here. I told you it was dead."

"Don't make me ask again. You already told me you had one."

"But it's dead. I left it in the car. Under the driver's seat."

"Why'd you hide it?"

"Didn't want to tempt anyone who might happen along."

Luther motioned with the gun at the man. "You first. In the basement."

Keeping his hands in the air, the man walked past her, not meeting her eyes. Then he was in the basement. The second he was in, Luther pushed her in behind him. She fell on top of him. His arms were the only thing that kept her from falling down the steps. A moment later the door slammed shut, leaving them in darkness.

6

She crumpled to the floor as she pulled away him, unable to stop the sobs.

His hand touched her shoulder. "It'll be OK."

"He's going to kill both of us. You shouldn't have tried to help me."

"That won't happen. Trust me."

"I don't see how you can say that. He'll move your car and then come back to kill us. Why didn't you just shoot him? Even if he did shoot me, you wouldn't have died."

"Nobody's dying. God won't let that happen."

"I don't see how He'll stop it."

"Because I really am a cop, and when my boss doesn't hear from me, she'll call in the cavalry."

"You're a cop? I thought you told him you weren't."

"I lied."

"It will still be too late. He's a...he's a horrible man. He'll probably kill you quickly, but he'll make me suffer." More sobs. "Even more than he already has."

"Have a little faith." He knelt down and hugged her closer to him.

His kindness made more tears flow. She became aware of the wetness of his shirt. "You're hurt."

"I don't think it's too bad. It feels as if the bleeding's already stopped. And I'm not dizzy or anything. Not now anyway. If I hadn't passed out back there, this whole thing would have gone differently. So I'm the one who's sorry." He maneuvered around her as he stood.

"Don't leave me."

"We need to get out of here."

A moment later, she heard the crash of his boot on the door. "Ouch. I think it's a steel door."

Another crash.

"Definitely a steel door. We aren't getting out that way. Is there another way out? In the basement?"

"I don't know. This is the first he's even let me out of the room." She stood and felt the wall, flicking a switch. A dim light came on below them. "Too bad your phone's not working. We could call for help."

"Another mistake on my part. I shouldn't have left it in the car."

"If he finds it, will he be able to tell you're a cop?"

"I took the battery out, but the computer will be a dead giveaway. But maybe he won't find the computer. Glad I took the time to hide it."

"Oh, he'll find it."

"See if you can find a weapon of some sort while I keep trying to kick down the door. Maybe there's another way out of here. Sometimes farm houses have an outside entrance to the basement. Look around."

She stared into the basement, horror seeping in. But he was right. There had to be something they could use as a weapon. Holding on to the rail, heart hammering, she made her way down the steps and back into her prison. Fear threatened to engulf her. She needed a distraction.

"What's your name?" Her voice was trembling and weak.

"Nate." Another kick at the door. "I'm a cop from

Mt. Pleasant."

"Really? Luther said nobody was looking for me." She searched around the dark room, not seeing anything that could be helpful. "I thought he might be right."

"Your cousin came in today. She's very worried about you."

Grateful tears slid down her cheeks. Keren. Someone cared enough. Luther was wrong. Someone did love her. Her gaze scanned the bare room. "Nothing down here at all. The room's completely empty. I guess Luther wanted to make sure there were no weapons down here just in case I got out of the room. I don't see any other way out." She made her way back up the steps.

"I don't think this thing's coming down. He probably made sure it would keep his secrets safe."

"I can't believe you're here. You came for me." She trembled and swayed toward him, her muscles feeling weak.

He grabbed her by the shoulders. "Don't fall apart now. We've got to find a way out of here."

"We won't. He's a madman." Her voice sounded hysterical even to her, but she couldn't stop. "He's…going to…ki…kill us."

His arms went around her. "God won't let that happen. It's not your time or mine. Let's go."

"Where?"

"He'll be expecting us up here ready to jump him. We need to throw him off his game. Not make things easy for him." His arm looped through hers as they went down into the basement. "I can't believe there's no kind of weapon down here. Not even a rake or shovel."

"I can't..." Her mind clicked. "Of course there's weapons. His tools. I forgot." She tugged him toward her prison. She stopped at the doorway. "In there. He's got...all sorts of things."

~*~

Things? Nate hurried past her. The first thing he saw was the bed... and the bloodstains. Dear God, what had that man done to her? To his left was a long table. His stomach twisted as he walked over.

Knives of all sizes and shapes, scalpels, and an array of other surgical-looking tools. In the right hands, the items were life-saving. In the wrong hands...his stomach turned. Nate didn't even want to think about what Luther had done to that poor woman. No wonder she was terrified of Luther Marks. What had she endured?

He grabbed the largest two knives and a hammer. He had to be ready for Luther.

Ange wouldn't look at him.

Even in the dim light, Nate could see the flush of her face. "It doesn't matter what he did. None of it was your fault and you survived. That's all that matters."

"So far."

"And we'll keep on surviving. We need to find a place to hide before he gets back."

"I wonder what's taking him so long."

"It was a long walk to my car. I left it on the side of the road, but he'll be back soon. We need to be ready." He handed her a knife.

Not moving, she stared at the weapon and then

took a step backward. "I can't."

"Yes, you can. It's not wrong to kill in self-defense. And we're in a battle for our lives." He handed it to her. "Take it. And use it if necessary."

She grabbed it, but he was pretty sure she wouldn't be able to use it when the time came. Protecting her would be up to him. *Please God, help me keep her safe.* In the dim light, he scanned the room. She was right–no other way out that he could see. No storm door. Just a typical basement, other than the fact it was completely bare.

Luther hadn't wanted to give his victims any type of weapons in case they got out of the room. Of course, he hadn't thought about his own tools. Strange.

"Under the stairs."

He reached up and unscrewed the light bulb. The sudden darkness made her gasp. "Sorry, I guess I should have warned you." He took hold of her arm and guided her under the steps. "This is actually a great spot. As he walks down, I might be able to grab his feet and make him fall. If that happens, we need to move quick. You run up the steps and out of the house and I'll be right behind you."

"Sounds like a plan."

"And you don't stop. No matter what happens. Understand? You keep running away from this house."

"But—"

"No buts. You run up those steps and out of this house. And you keep running to the road and get as far away from here as you can. As quick as you can. Don't look back or worry about me. I can take care of myself. Got it?"

"You said you'd be right behind me."

"And that's probably true. But just in case that doesn't happen, you keep running until you find help. Promise me you'll leave. Without me."

There was silence for a moment. "I can't just leave you."

"Yes, you can. I can take care of myself. And I'll be able to do that a whole lot better if I'm not worrying about you. Promise me. Please."

"I promise."

He nudged her with his shoulder. "Good. And don't even think about breaking that promise."

7

Ange leaned against him, taking comfort from his physical presence. She felt safe with him. Luther Marks wanted both of them dead. And this man was intent on protecting her despite not knowing her at all. If he died, it would be her fault. "What did you say your name was again? I forgot."

"It's Nate. Nate Goodman."

"That's a good name for you because you are a good man."

"Thanks."

"And you're really from Mt. Pleasant?"

"Born and bred."

"I never met you before, did I?"

"Not that I can remember."

"I...I went to private schools. I didn't know many people from the town."

"We all know about you, though. You're our claim to fame."

"A lot of good that did me." She'd thought being famous was the most important thing in the world. But life was more important—and freedom.

Would Nate be able to fight Luther off with just a knife? Probably not. In the end, Luther would still win, but at least she'd die knowing someone had tried to help her and that Keren had missed her. Someone cared about her. Luther was wrong. She wiped at the tears coursing down her cheeks. This all was so wrong.

"Are you sure this will work?"

"Not really. But it's the only idea I have. If you have a better one, I'd love to hear it."

Nate shouldn't die because of her. "I'm so sorry."

"Sorry? For what?"

"For getting you into this mess."

"You didn't get me in a mess. It's Luther Marks' fault. And only his fault. No matter what happens, you remember that. This is not your fault."

"But—"

"But nothing. Not your fault. I don't care what you did or didn't do to get you in this situation. It's still Luther Marks' fault. And only his."

She was silent, mulling over what he'd said in her mind.

"Whose fault is it?"

She smiled in the darkness. "Luther's."

"Now you got it. And don't forget—" He stopped abruptly as footsteps approached above them.

He was back. She clenched his arm.

He leaned in and whispered, "God keep us safe. Amen."

"Amen."

The door opened.

"And don't forget your promise," Nate whispered.

He moved away from her. Even though she couldn't see him, she knew what he was doing. Getting in position to grab Luther's feet. Please let his idea work.

"Both of you get up here. Now." Luther's voice was breathless, terrified. "You don't really think you can hide from me, do you? I'm the one in control. I won't say it again. Get up here. Now. Or you'll be sorry."

Ange stayed quiet. But to her surprise she found a part of her actually wanted to go up the steps like he'd ordered her to do. She fought the urge to comply.

Luther's breathing was heavy as he stood at the top of the steps.

She touched Nate's back to reassure herself that he was really there. She wasn't alone.

"If you come up, I'll make it easy on you." Luther almost sounded pleasant. "If not, you'll suffer more than you can imagine."

She didn't have to imagine what that meant. She'd been living it since he'd locked her in this basement. Still she smiled in the darkness because Luther didn't want to come down those steps to find them. He was afraid.

That was a victory. A small one, but still a victory.

"By the way, I found your phone. But the battery was missing. No wonder it wouldn't work. What are you trying to hide from me, Nathan? Yes, I know your name, and it won't take me long to figure out exactly who you are."

He didn't mention the computer. What would he do when he found out Nate really was a cop? Try to escape or try to kill them? Probably both. Kill them and then escape.

His footsteps moved away.

Was he leaving? Hope bubbled inside Ange's heart. Maybe he really would go away. Just leave them and try to escape. So he wouldn't get arrested. Her hope faded as quickly as it had bloomed.

A moment later Luther's footsteps came back.

A bright flashlight moved down into the darkness. The light scanned the steps. Hopefully, Luther couldn't see Nate standing below ready to grab his feet. The old wood squeaked with Luther's weight as he moved slowly down the steps.

Nate touched her shoulder. His signal for her to get ready to run.

The creaking stopped. Luther waited. Then moved down another step.

Ange couldn't breathe. Every muscle trembled. Another squeak. Another step. Silently, she moved away from Nate readying to run.

Luther's darkened shape was visible between the slats. But he was moving deliberately slow.

She didn't think Nate would be able to surprise him enough to trip him.

Time crawled as they waited.

"You might as well come out now. This little game will backfire on both of you. Ange, you can't escape. There's no use in trying. You're making me very angry. And you know what that means, Ange."

One more step and he'd be within Nate's range.

The cone of light scanned the area.

"Fine. I'm done with this game." More squeaking as Luther moved up the steps and away from Nate's hands. The light disappeared leaving them in complete darkness. "I'll just lock you in and wait for you both to die. What do I care? There's no way for you to get out of here. You can just starve to death for all I care."

The door slammed shut—their death knell.

She slid to the floor, sobbing.

A moment later, Nate was beside her, his arms around her. "Don't worry. We've got him freaked out. You know what that means?"

She shook her head but he couldn't see her. "No."

"It gives us more time for my boss to come rescue us. And it means Luther will start making mistakes.

Actually, he already made his first mistake."

"He did?"

"Yep, kidnapping you was his first mistake. He just didn't know it at the time."

"Yeah, right."

"Right as rain. Maybe that first plan didn't work, but I guarantee you he'll not just keep us locked up here until we die from starvation. Sooner or later, he'll come back, and we'll be ready for him."

"Why not? It's actually a good plan. Just leave us down here to die."

"It is, but we've taken control from him. Men like Luther don't like that. I guarantee he'll want to take it back. And sooner, rather than later."

"But we're not giving it to him."

"That's the spirit. And even if he doesn't come back that's OK. It gives my boss more time to find us. Win-win for us."

She leaned against Nate. "I'm so glad you're here with me, Nate."

He hugged her. "Me, too."

"That's nice of you to say, but I'm sure it's not true."

"It is very true. There's no place I'd rather be than here with you."

"That's crazy. I wouldn't want to be here if I could help it. I'd rather be anywhere but here. Even in jail."

"It's not crazy at all. It's my job to find you, and I'm glad I did. If I hadn't found you, you might not have survived. But together, we'll survive. I promise. God has our back on this one."

"I don't know how you can be so optimistic."

"God. Because of God."

"I wish I could believe that, too. But God doesn't

love me. And I don't blame Him. I actually prayed today for Him to help me, but He didn't hear me."

"Of course, He did. That's why I'm here. It only proves that He loves you very much, Ange. And it's all going to work out because I know something you don't know."

"What's that?"

"I keep telling you. Sooner or later, my boss will come looking for me. And it will probably be sooner. She's not much for patience. So expect her to show up any second."

"I hope you're right."

"I am."

She leaned against him feeling safer than she had since this nightmare started. She wasn't alone in the dark any more. *God, is Nate the answer to my prayer? Did You really hear me? Is Nate right? Do You still love me?*

~*~

Ange's head drooped to his shoulder, and her breathing turned even. She must be asleep. That was probably a good thing. If she could get away from this reality for even a few minutes by sleeping, she deserved it.

It was hard to imagine what she'd endured at the hands of Luther Marks, the bruises and cuts on her body that he could see were sickening. Nate shuddered at the evilness of the man's tools. The sick, depraved mind that had used them filled him with disgust.

Nate hoped Leslie would call in backup. A lot of it. How much time had passed since he'd called Leslie?

An hour? Two? Surely long enough for her to convince the proper authorities that he was in trouble. What if she couldn't convince them? No, he wouldn't think like that. *I know You've got my back, God.* Leslie wouldn't just abandon him. This wasn't a broken engagement. This was part of his job, and hers. Leslie always did the right thing. And she would this time, too. But how long would it take—and would they still be alive when she got here?

Luther was stomping around upstairs, no doubt trying to figure out what he should do. Each of those stomps meant he was getting more and more aggravated. And angrier. It would be Luther's undoing. He was too mad now to think about the fact that he should be escaping. And there was no way Luther would just let them stay in the basement until they died. Luther wouldn't be that patient. He'd be back. And from the sounds overhead, it wouldn't be long. The stomping was growing more frequent and stronger.

Nate needed to be ready when Luther opened that door.

~*~

A scrabbling sound accompanied a soft groan. Ange must have awoken and the sudden movement hurt her.

"Ange." His voice was soft but reassuring. "Don't be afraid. It's Nate."

She wasn't alone in the dark again. Nate was here. "What's wrong?"

"Nothing's wrong. But we need to be ready. Have another surprise waiting for Mr. Marks when he opens that door the next time."

Through her grogginess, she became aware of a lot of stomping going on up above.

"It won't be too long before he comes back for us."

Her stomach lurched. "What will we do?"

"The unexpected. He'll assume we'll still be down here hiding, but I'll be on the landing waiting when he opens that door."

"Is that a good idea? He has a gun."

"The element of surprise. I'll get the drop on him before he has a chance to use his gun. I want you to wait down here, but the first chance you get, run up the steps and out of here. Just as we discussed before. OK?"

She didn't say anything.

"OK? Same idea as before. You go get help."

"I hate—"

"You promised. And I really need you to get out of here and go find some help."

"I thought you said your boss would send someone to help."

"And she will as soon as she figures out I need help. In the meantime, we help ourselves. So you're running up the steps, and you'll get out of this house. Right?"

"Fine, but I'm not happy about it."

"As long as you do it, that's OK with me. I'll go up by the door. You wait down here as close to the steps as you can get without being seen."

"Maybe I should go up with you."

"No, let's just stick with my plan."

He didn't want her in the line of fire. Why would

anyone be willing to die? For her? Tears crowded her eyes. "OK."

The moment he walked away, a knife in his hand, she felt alone. She stood. Both of her feet had fallen asleep. In the darkness, she quietly moved from side to side, hoping she'd be ready. She moved toward the bottom of the steps and waited. The air shifted, something was about to happen. She could feel it.

Without warning, light came from above as Luther opened the door. The moment the light shone in, the struggle started. Heavy breathing. A moan or a groan as they fought. More bumping. Luther cussing. But no gunshots. Yet.

She moved closer to the steps.

The two shadowed figures were entangled with each other. Who was who? Who was winning? Even with the light from the kitchen, all she could see were shadows. One of the shadows stumbled and then fell backward. The other shadow pushed against his chest. The falling shadow tumbled down the steps toward her.

Nate? Or Luther?

The shadow became a man as he landed near her. Luther. His eyes were open as he reached for her.

She stared, terrified, and then her mind snapped a warning. She charged up the steps.

"Run." Nate yelled at her as she reached the top. "Keep running."

She grabbed his arm. "You too. You gotta come with me."

He gave her a little push out of the stairwell. "I can't. I have to finish this. Go without me. You promised."

She didn't want to leave him, but she nodded. She

pounded through the living room, still scattered with broken glass. At the door, she stopped. Nate needed her. But he'd made her promise. She opened the door.

Her feet froze.

~*~

Nate charged down the basement steps two at a time praying the man didn't have time to recover from the fall. Luther stared up at him, already half off the ground in spite of the stab wound Nate had inflicted.

Their gazes locked in an unspoken battle.

Luther stood with a gun in his hand.

Without thinking, Nate launched himself off the steps toward Ange's nemesis and made a grab for Luther's gun. He missed the gun but not Luther.

Luther moaned as he landed on his back on the hard cement floor. Nate fought for traction as he pulled away. The two men grappled for the gun—and their lives. Winner took all.

Nate managed to straddle Luther and his first punch glanced off the man's chin.

Luther grunted as he tried to push Nate off.

Nate didn't work out day after day for nothing. It would take more than that to dislodge him. "Stop. It's over." Nate gasped and grabbed the man's flailing hand.

Luther's response was to punch Nate in the gut. As Nate doubled over in pain, Luther pushed Nate off. "It's over when I say it's over and not until." He crawled away his hands flailing on the floor, apparently in search of the weapon.

Nate lunged toward it, but as he reached, Luther kicked him in the head. Nate's shoulder slammed hard into the cement floor.

Luther crawled toward the gun.

He couldn't let him get it. Moving to his knees, Nate charged forward and slammed into Luther's back. Luther fell forward.

Nate's arm snaked around the fiend's throat. "It's over."

"I wouldn't count on that." The words came out as gasps.

"Then you'll die." His arm tightened around his opponent's neck.

"One of us will." Luther managed to stand, and in the process, he threw Nate off his back. "But it won't be me."

Luther had the gun aimed at Nate.

Luther's eyes bulged with rage. He fired.

Nate rolled away as the bullet slammed into the cement floor. Using the momentum from the roll, he managed to jump up. He charged at Luther, using his full force as he leaned down, and rammed into the man's stomach.

~*~

Ange couldn't believe her eyes.

Three police cars with red and blue lights whirling were in the yard. Why hadn't they come in yet to help Nate?

"Stop!" a voice commanded. "Don't move."

She moved her hands in a surrender position as

shown in the movies. "But you need—"

"Shut up and don't move." A huge man, well over six feet, walked toward her.

"But—"

Another police officer, a woman, jogged past the huge man. She stopped in front of Ange. "Where's Nate?"

"In the basement. He needs help. Hurry," she cried, still keeping her hands up in the air. The woman zoomed away. Ange called after her. "Be careful. Luther has a gun."

The woman pulled out her own gun. *Good.*

"I said don't move," the man repeated his command.

"I didn't do anything. I'm—"

"I know who you are. But we still need to do this step by step. So please don't—"

A gunshot. And then another.

He grabbed her by the shoulders and pushed her out of the way, yelling to another officer. "Take her. I'm going in." He disappeared into the house.

Another officer approached her. He held out his hand. "Let's get you somewhere safe."

Safe. Was she really safe? Really free? She hadn't thought it possible, but she'd survived Luther Marks. It was over. But what about Nate? *Please God, keep him safe.* Without Nate, she'd still be in Luther's torture chamber.

But he couldn't hurt her anymore.

She stared up at the house. And prayed to God, whom she'd not spoken to in years until this ordeal. "Please, please let Nate survive."

8

Nate walked into Ange Matthews' hospital room. His own arm was in a sling, but the doctor said there shouldn't be any permanent damage. The arm throbbed in spite of the painkillers the doctor had insisted on. But he didn't want to think about what he'd be feeling without them.

Ange was hooked up to a monitor and an IV. Her eyes were closed and her face was swollen and bruised around the cuts. Although he couldn't see them, he'd been told there were more cuts on her arms and legs, a testament to Luther's brutality. She'd been cut and beaten up on a daily basis during her captivity.

Keren sat in a chair beside her bed. She held Ange's hand. Her finger moved to her lips to hush him as she whispered. "She's sleeping."

"No, I'm not." Ange opened her eyes.

"Sorry. I didn't mean to disturb you." Nate stood in the doorway. "I just wanted to make sure you were OK before I left."

She smiled at him, transforming her face into the beauty that Luther had tried to steal. Even in her present condition, her loveliness shone through.

"How could you disturb me? You're my knight in shining armor. You rescued me." She grinned as she moved to a sitting position. "I was so worried about you. But they wouldn't let me see you. They brought me straight here."

"Yeah, some rescuer I turned out to be. The rescuer had to be rescued."

"Considering he had a gun and you didn't, I'd say you did a great job. I can't thank you enough for...for everything." Her voice trembled. "What can I do for you? Can I give you a reward?"

"No, you cannot. Just seeing you here alive and well is all the reward I need."

Her hand touched her swollen face. "I don't know how well, but I'm alive." She grinned. "Thanks to you, my hero."

"I'm not a hero. I was only doing my job. You're the hero." Nate moved to the foot of Ange's bed.

"Not me. You're the one who saved me and you know it. So stop the modest act. If you hadn't started checking on me, I'd still be in that filthy room." Her eyes closed, and he knew she was back there with Luther. She opened then and met his gaze. "Or dead. He'd told me he would kill me that night. And I believed him."

"Don't say that. Don't even think about it." Keren shook her head, looking distraught. "It's all over now. You never have to see that awful man again. Or even think about him."

"You should thank your cousin. She reported you missing. If she hadn't come in..." He shrugged. "Well, let's just say I'm glad she decided to."

"And you're the one who found me. I'm grateful to both of you."

"There you have it." Keren laughed. "We're all heroes."

"Especially you. For surviving. That couldn't have been an easy thing to go through." Nate's voice was soft.

"Well, it's all over now. She never has to think about any of it ever again." Keren hugged her cousin. "She can get on with her life."

That was easier said than done. He'd had his share of trauma as a marine, and then later as a Chicago cop. He only hoped Keren was right. Ange had suffered enough. "Are they done interviewing you?"

She nodded. "For now. They said I could get some rest and we'd start again in the morning." Her blue eyes gazed at him. "What happened to Luther? Did you…"

"Dead. Leslie shot him. When she'd come down those steps, Luther could have given up. Instead he pointed the gun at her. And then it was over."

"Good. That's what he deserved," Keren said.

Luther's death saddened him. As long as he was alive, the man had a chance to find God. Now that chance was gone. But that had been his decision. Not Leslie's or Nate's.

"At least he won't be able to hurt anyone else. Did…did they…find anyone else there? You know what I mean. Anyone…" Ange swallowed. "Anyone dead?"

"The FBI's searching his property. They were called in because this deals with a kidnapping, and at least two states are involved in the case. Could be more. He liked to move around. Didn't stay any place for longer than a year or two. Last I heard there are missing women from every town he lived in. Of course, that doesn't mean he's responsible."

"But I'm sure he is. At least for some of them." Ange's eyes glazed over. She was, again, back in that room with Luther.

"He can't hurt you anymore. You're safe."

"That's right," her cousin said. "He can't hurt you anymore, Ange."

"Don't call me Ange. I never want to hear that name again. Ever."

Her cousin blinked at the vehemence in Ange's voice.

Nothing was over for this poor woman. She'd been through so much. If the instruments that had been found in that room were any indication, it would be a long time before she'd forget—if ever. It would take time to heal—both physically and emotionally.

"But that's your name. What do you want me to call you, then?" Keren asked.

"Call me Angelina. That's my real name, remember?" Her voice was grim.

"If you say so."

He smiled at her. "Angelina. I like it. That's a beautiful name, just like its owner."

She shook her head. "I'm not beautiful. I'm…I'm…" Tears streamed down her face. Her words were lost in her sobs.

Keren looked at Nate then put her arms around her cousin. "Ange…Angelina. Don't cry. It's all over. You're safe now."

Angelina looked up at Nate. "I'll never feel safe again."

"It will take some time, Angelina, but you'll be able to put this nightmare behind you. Someday. I promise."

"If you say so." Her mouth lifted, not really a smile, through her tears.

9

"Hey, Chief." Diane, one of his co-workers, stopped at his desk.

"What's up, Diane?" Nate looked up from the form he was filling out, one of many.

"Just wanted to let you know I happened to drive past The Matthews estate earlier. I couldn't believe it."

"Believe what?"

"It looks bad. The grass looks as if it hasn't been mown in weeks."

"That's not against the law."

"I know that. It looks as if it's been abandoned. That got me thinking."

"About what?"

"How she is—if she's OK." Diane leaned against his door. "I'm just worried about her, you know. She went through a lot. I know she doesn't have much family."

Diane didn't have to say who the she was. Ange— Angelina Matthews. Her kidnapping and rescue had made the national news, and it had been fodder for local gossip for the past four months.

"She was OK the last time I saw her, but that's been months ago. She was still in the hospital then." After all the trauma she'd suffered, she probably wasn't OK.

"I actually hung around with her some when we were kids. My mom worked for them so we'd play together sometimes. She was nice. A little spoiled, but still nice. Just thought maybe you'd want to check on her."

"Why me?"

"Why not? You're her hero. That's what she told all the papers." Diane grinned.

"I don't know about all that. But still it might be a good idea. Thanks for the update."

"No problem, Chief. Or should I call you Mr. Hero?"

"Nate will do just fine." He tossed a paper clip at her as she walked away.

Nate stared at his ever-growing mountain of paperwork. He hadn't become a policeman so he could spend his days behind a desk. But with Leslie's departure, he'd become chief, and all his time seemed to be spent doing exactly that. He was sure his part in the rescue of Angelina Matthews was the deciding factor in his new job. He tapped the desk with a pen. He had to deal with this, but not right now. He should get out from behind this desk. Of course, checking on Angelina Matthews wasn't exactly police work. But he could make sure she was all right—if she needed anything.

She'd been through so much trauma. It was difficult to get back to a normal life after such an ordeal. He probably should have checked on her sooner. Within seconds, he had his hat and keys to one of the cruisers in his hand. He'd just take a drive around town, and head out that way.

Going down the long driveway to the Matthews' home, he was appalled.

Diane had been polite when she'd said the lawn needed mowed. It needed harvesting, probably with some type of heavy farm equipment. The average lawn mower couldn't deal with this brush. Angelina must be in a bad place for her not to notice the unkempt aura of neglect. She could pay for the best of services.

But then, he knew personally how hard it could be to trust anyone she might hire.

Nate parked in front of the mansion. The red brick circular drive led to a matching thirty-foot red brick walk. On both sides stood huge cement pillars so no one would drive on the walk. The house was brick as well, the same shade as the sidewalk leading up to it. There were stripes of decorative white bricks at both ends that broke up the red. The white bricks also surrounded the windows, making it seem as if there were shutters. To the right of the house was a matching building, but smaller, although it was still huge. A garage? It was more elaborate than any garage or storage unit he'd been in. It looked to be two stories. He glanced back at the house. The main house had three stories.

He stepped out of his car and walked up to the door. Shoots of green were popping up between the bricks. Another sign that the house and lawn weren't being cared for. The entire place had an empty feeling as if it had been abandoned. He rang the buzzer several times. No sounds came from inside, except the intricate chimes of the doorbell. He glanced around at the desolation again.

Angelina wasn't here.

Where was she? Why wasn't she taking care of her home?

It wasn't his business. But he sighed, knowing he didn't really believe that. One of his life verses was Second Corinthians, verse one. "And the God of all comfort who comforts us in all our troubles, so that we can comfort those in any trouble with the comfort we ourselves receive from God."

Nate took the Bible very seriously. Scripture was part of the reason he'd become a police officer. God had helped him through several traumatic events. His calling was to return the favor for others.

And from the looks of this place, Angelina Matthews might be in need of God's comfort.

~*~

Two hours later, Nate pulled up in front of a tiny house in the Old Brooklyn neighborhood of Cleveland. Its lawn was well-maintained, unlike the Matthews' home.

He'd gone back to the station and looked up Keren's address on the missing person's form she'd filled out. If Angelina wasn't staying at her own house, she might be with her cousin.

He walked up the steps and rang the doorbell. When he heard nothing inside, he knocked. Maybe the buzzer was broken. He probably should have called but something prodded him to act, so he did.

"Who is it?" A woman called from the other side, reminding him of when Luther Marks had done the same.

"It's Nate Goodman. From Mt. Pleasant."

The door opened and Keren smiled at him. "Well, yes, it is. What are you doing here, Officer Goodman?"

He didn't tell her he was the chief now. "I came to check on Angelina. See how she's doing."

Her eyes widened.

Maybe he should have called first.

"She's doing just fine. You could have saved yourself a trip and just called me to ask."

"I don't mean to be rude, but actually, I came to see her. To see how she's doing with my own eyes."

"Oh…I see. In that case, you definitely wasted a trip to Cleveland. She's not seeing anyone quite yet." She maintained a smile.

Quite yet. It had been four months. That wasn't a lot of time, but she should be recuperated enough to be seeing people.

"You don't think she'll see me? She did call me her hero." He reminded.

Keren smiled, but her voice was firm. "She says she doesn't want to see people right now. I'm trying to respect what she wants. To give her the time and space she needs. But I'll tell her you stopped by."

"Ask her if she wants to see me while I'm still here."

She sighed. "I suppose I can do that, but I don't think it will do any good. She refuses to see anyone. Even Zarlengo, when he came."

"Thanks."

She opened the door wider. "You might as well come in while you wait."

The living room was tiny and obviously not used. Just an uncomfortable looking sofa and a matching chair with a fake fireplace. And neat as a pin.

Keren went up the stairs. Her body language clearly showed she wasn't happy about his insistence. She looked back at him with a worried expression.

He wanted to see Angelina with his own eyes, and that sudden importance to do so surprised him.

Muted voices sounded from upstairs.

Keren appeared on the landing. "She said to come on up."

He went up and knocked on the door that Keren pointed at.

"Come on in."

He opened the door. "Hey."

"Hey back." She sat on the bed cross-legged. "Sorry I'm in my pajamas. I wasn't expecting any company."

"Not a problem. I guess I should have called before I came, but I sort of just decided up on a whim." He spied a chair in the corner of the room. "Mind if I sit down for a bit so we can visit?"

She nodded.

She didn't look well. Her hair was stringy, and undyed roots had grown out a several inches. The dark circles under her eyes indicated she probably wasn't sleeping either.

"Angelina, I know we don't really know each other but..." He paused trying to decide how to bring up a difficult topic.

"You can say anything you want to me. You earned that right when you saved my life. So just say what you want to say."

"You don't look as if you're doing well. I can understand that. You went through a lot while you were trapped in that house. But you're not trapped there anymore."

"I know that. Thanks to you."

"But it looks as if you might still be imprisoned."

"I don't know what you mean." She played with the edge of the quilt.

"Luther Marks stole a few weeks of your life. He's

gone now. He can't hurt you again. Don't let him steal anything else from you. Like your future. Don't give him that power."

"But there are others out there like him." Her voice was so soft he strained to hear her words. "He wasn't the only bad person in the world, you know."

"That's true, but you can't let that stop you from living your life. You can't get stuck in all the bad things that could happen. Don't let yourself get trapped in another prison." He motioned around the room. "Don't let this room become your prison."

She looked up, tears glistening. "It's not my prison. It's my sanctuary."

"Get dressed." He understood her feelings, but the cycle of imprisonment had to stop.

"Why?"

"Because I drove all the way up here to see you, and I'm really hungry. And you probably don't want to go out in your PJs, do you? What would people think if you did such a shocking thing?" He grinned, hoping to lighten her mood.

She smiled but shook her head. "I...I'm just not ready to go out in public. To face people. My face was all over the news. Now when people look at me, they'll know."

"They know you're a survivor. That you were brave enough not to give up. Brave enough to not run when you had the chance. Instead, you stayed and helped me after I was shot. If you hadn't hit him with that frying pan, I probably would be dead now. That's what people remember."

She wiped away tears. "I wish that was true."

"It is true."

"Luther Marks was right when he said I was

worthless. That my life was worthless."

"God doesn't create worthless."

"What have I done then?" Her voice held a challenge. "Other than to be born to wealthy parents? I've spent my whole life spending their money. I've done nothing to be proud of."

"You survived a serial killer. And stopped him from killing any more women."

"That was because of you. Not me."

"It was both of us. And maybe you're right when you say you haven't done a whole lot. Yet. But you're still breathing. The Bible says a righteous man gets back up seven times. And it's time for you to get up."

"There's nothing righteous about me, so I guess I don't have to get back up." She patted the bed. "I'll stay here. It's comfortable and safe. Nobody can get me here."

"You're not a Christian?"

"I guess I am. I trusted Him a long time ago. I've...I've done so many..." She hung her head, her words lost in her sobs. "Bad things. God probably hates me."

"God loves you. And a long time ago or not, that means you're righteous in God's eyes. And you know what that means?"

"You always talk about God as if He's in the room. As if He's your best friend."

"I guess that's a good way to describe my relationship with God. He is with me all the time. But He's with you, too.

"No, He's not."

"You told me you prayed to God that day. The same day Keren came to the station to tell me you were missing. That's not just a coincidence. That was God working on your behalf."

"I don't think so."

"I know so, and what's more, He's right here waiting for you still. And you know what that means, right?

She didn't answer but looked at him as if waiting for the answer.

"That means it's time to get back—"

"You need to leave her alone." Keren charged through the open door. She glared at him as she rushed to Angelina's side. "Stop badgering her. She doesn't want to go anywhere with you. She's fine here. With me."

"I'm not badgering. I'm—"

"Why are you even here? I'm taking care of her. She doesn't need you. And you sure aren't helping."

Angelina pulled away from her cousin. "Actually, he is. I think he's right. I can't just lay in this bed forever. Hiding out in your house."

"Of course not forever. But until you're ready." Keren's voice was soothing, but the look she gave Nate wasn't. "When you're ready, you'll get back in the swing of things. You just need a little more time. And he doesn't need to bother you."

"He's not bothering me." Angelina stood. "Guess I'm ready. And I'm hungry."

Keren glared at him as she took a step away from Angelina. "If that's what you want to do, Angelina, that's fine with me. I'm not trying to stop you from doing anything. I just didn't want him badgering you."

Angelina genuinely smiled at him. "If you'll excuse me while I get dressed. Pajamas may be comfortable but they definitely aren't dinner clothes."

"Sure." He grinned and followed Keren out of the

room.

"I really don't think this is a good idea," Keren whispered outside the door. "You haven't been around her. You just don't understand."

"Maybe not but hiding out in your house isn't a good idea either."

She went down the stairs, her back stiff with disapproval.

He sat down on the steps.

A few minutes later, Angelina walked out. Her hair was pulled back in a ponytail. She had on jeans and a T-shirt, nothing fancy. The jeans were loose. She'd lost weight since the last time he'd seen her.

She took a deep breath. "Is this…OK?"

"You look beautiful."

She grinned. "If you say so." She stared down at the first step, her expression pensive.

"What's going on?"

"Nothing. Nothing. I'm fine."

He wasn't so sure about that. He looped his arm through hers as they moved down the steps. "Great. So, what are you in the mood for?"

"In the mood for?"

"To eat."

"Oh." She seemed surprised, as if she'd forgotten what they were doing.

Keren sat in one of the uncomfortable looking easy chairs. Her expression was worried. "Anything's fine with me," Angelina said. "There's a Mexican restaurant down the street that's good." Her voice squeaked. Her face was splotched with red and her breathing was uneven.

"Are you sure you're OK?"

Angelina nodded, but her gaze was on the door.

"Nice to see you again," he said to Keren. "I'll have her home early."

Keren's gaze was glued on Angelina.

He opened the door.

Angelina froze. Her breathing turned ragged. "I...uh...I...I..."

"Angelina." He gently tapped her chin to bring her face up so he could meet her gaze. "How long has it been since you left the house?"

"Since I got here," her voice was a mere whisper.

"You mean you haven't gone anywhere since then? At all?"

She nodded, but her gaze stayed focused on the door. "Didn't seem to be a reason to."

This was worse than he'd imagined. "OK. No problem. I can understand that you're a little anxious, but you're with me. I won't let anyone hurt you."

"I know. I know that."

"OK, then. We can do this. Just one step at a time. Baby steps."

"Right. Baby steps." She moved toward the door.

He walked around her and held open the screen. "Take your time. You're doing great."

She scrunched her forehead in hard concentration, her face bright red. Her foot touched the last piece of carpet before the door, and she stopped.

No one spoke.

Keren's expression was triumphant. She met his gaze as if to say, 'I knew this was going to happen.' She shrugged.

"Angelina, if you can't—"

She wasn't listening. An internal battle was being waged. She was wringing her hands as she took a step backward. "I can't. I can't. I can't. I'm sorry but I just can't do it."

"It's OK. You're allowed to change your mind. It's not a problem at all. I'll go get us some takeout. We can eat here. It's fine."

She focused on the floor. "It's not fine. I...I...I'm such a mess. Such a failure." She wiped at the tears coursing down her cheeks.

"You are no such thing. We can do this another time. It's not a big deal." He reached out to her. "You made it this far, and that's a giant step forward."

Angelina fell to her knees, her head on the floor as she sobbed. After a few moments, she looked up at him. She reached out. "Help me."

10

"You didn't have to come to check up on me. I told you I'd take Angelina to her doctor's appointment." Keren glared at Nate as they stood out on her porch once again. "And I will. But I sure don't know why you picked one so far away."

"Because she's the best." Why did this woman dislike him? He'd been the only one who'd believed her when she'd told them Angelina was missing. Nate forced a smile. "And I do trust you. That's not why I'm here. I knew you would do what you said."

"Even though I disagree with it?" Keren shook her head. "She doesn't need a doctor. She needs time. There's nothing wrong with her that being around a loving family can't cure."

"I agree. She does need you. But sometimes we need a little more than family to get through a difficult time." He knew that from experience. "You gave me your word so I believed you. I just thought Angelina could use a little extra support today. I saw what happened when she tried to leave before. I wanted to be here to encourage her."

Keren's gaze flicked toward the steps. "Oh." Her burst of anger seemed to deflate. "I'm sorry. I'm a little anxious. We all are. Peter even took some time off. He'll meet us at the clinic."

"Good. She needs both of you supporting her."

"It's just…I don't know. I knew it wasn't good for

her to just hide out here. But at least she was safe. You know? And I didn't want to pressure her. Try to make her do something she didn't want to do."

He nodded.

"I come from a small family so...so I hate the thought of anything happening to her."

"Something did happen to her."

She nodded, her eyes filling with tears. "I know. But she survived it. And...in my family, we learned to just keep moving forward when something bad happened. Not to dwell on it."

"That's wonderful, but sometimes people get trapped in the bad times. Then they need a little help setting themselves free."

"I guess." She opened the screen door and motioned at the sofa. "Might as well get comfortable. Who knows how long—"

"Don't even finish that sentence, Keren. I'm ready." Angelina looked better. She was dressed and had washed her hair, but her face was still splotched with red, a sure sign she was anxious. "Morning, Nate."

"You look great."

"Liar." She walked to the middle of the living room. "But thanks for saying it anyway."

"I'm not—"

"Have you never seen a picture of me before?"

"I'm just saying you look good."

She took a deep breath as she stared at the open door. "OK, let's get this show on the road. I've got my nerve up but don't know how much longer that will last." She looked at Keren. "Even if I freak out, I want to go see the doctor. OK. You take me whether I want to go or not. Even if you have to pull me out of this house, I want to go."

"OK. But—"

"But you won't freak out." Nate smiled as he looped his arm through hers. "God's still got your back."

"I hope so." She took a deep breath and stopped one step before the porch.

"You can do this, Angelina," Nate said firmly. *Give her strength, God.*

She shook her head. Her eyes filled with tears. "I don't...think I can."

"Will you let Luther Marks win?"

One small tear traced its way down her cheek.

He fought the urge to wipe it away. He wanted to wrap her in his arms and make all her problems disappear. Instead, he smiled. "Then let's not let him. One baby step outside. That's all you need to do. One baby step."

She took a deep breath. "One baby step." Her foot moved forward. And then she was outside.

"All-righty! You did the hardest part."

She had a long road ahead. If she learned to lean on God, she'd make it.

She took a deep breath and then looked back at Keren. "Lock the door before I can change my mind. I've got an appointment I plan to keep"

~*~

Angelina opened the door marked Conference. It had been more than three weeks since Nate and Keren had brought her to the clinic. Turned out that she wasn't crazy. Her diagnosis had been PTSD. She wasn't in the loony bin; she was at the clinic. The euphemisms went on and on. A post-hospitalization plan, her doctor called it. A plan to keep her out of the hospital and healthy. If she didn't succeed, would they lock her up forever? A part of her thought it might be for the best — at least she'd be safe.

Wrong attitude. Nate would be disappointed with her. Not that what he thought mattered. She hadn't even heard from him since she came to the clinic — and she thought she would. Apparently, he'd done his good deed for the week.

That was fine. She had her own life to live. She didn't need Nate Goodman. Or anyone. Still, she'd thought he'd been sincere when he'd told her that he cared.

As she walked into the conference room, Keren jumped up from the table and rushed over to her. She put her arms around Angelina. "How are you, sweetie? It's so good to finally see you. I've been so worried. I wanted to come to sooner, but the doctors told me to wait until you felt better."

Felt better. Another euphemism. "Then I guess that means I'm better since you're here." Maybe Nate had been told the same thing.

Keren's husband, Peter, smiled at her. She hadn't liked Peter when he'd married Keren, but she'd been wrong. He'd been kind to her since the kidnapping and hadn't asked for a thing in return. Not even money to help out.

Now it was time for everyone to sit around and decide what was best for her. They pretended as if she had a say in the matter.

Dr. Markley stood. She didn't look much like a

doctor even with the white smock. Her long blonde hair hung down below her shoulders. Under the smock was a flowing flowered skirt with a soft blue top. "Good morning, Angelina. How are you feeling today?"

"Fine." She'd keep her answers short. The less she said the less chance to say the wrong thing.

The doctor motioned for her to sit opposite from Keren and Peter. "If you're like most of my patients, you hate this type of meeting. It feels as if we're deciding your life for you, but that's not what we're doing. We just want to get things organized so you have an easy transition."

And I don't end up back in the loony bin...oops, the clinic. Angelina sat down.

The doctor got right to the point. "So, what are your plans? After you get out."

"I don't know. Haven't thought about it. I'm not sure I'm ready to leave." Being in here was safer than being out there. "Maybe I should stay for a few months instead of a few weeks. I really don't mind."

The doctor nodded as if that meant something important then jotted on her notepad.

Angelina hated when the doctors did that. They always seemed so serious, so full of gloom and doom. As if every word she said had deep, psychological meaning.

Dr. Markley smiled as she looked up from the file. "I believe you're ready. I know it's scary out there. But once you understand that you're safe, that not everybody is out to hurt you, you'll be fine."

Why was it so hard for them to understand that if it happened once, it could happen again? Surely there were more serial killers out there waiting. Her fame brought them out, gave them opportunity to stalk and terrorize her. But Angelina only nodded.

Dr. Markley looked at Keren and Peter. "Angelina and I have had a few discussions about the fact she needs to regain her independence as well as find her place in the world."

"What's that mean?" Keren asked.

"I'll let Angelina tell you."

Angelina looked at Keren. "It means I can't live with you forever. I'm sure you're happy to hear that."

"We don't mind at all. You haven't been a bother. Right, Peter?"

He leaned forward with his elbows on the table. "Right. You've been the perfect house guest. Not a problem at all. We love having you stay with us."

"Thanks for saying that, but sooner or later, I need to move back home. I guess." She looked over at Dr. Markley, who smiled her agreement. "But maybe not quite yet. And I'm getting a job. I've spent my life doing nothi—"

"That's not true." Keren voiced with fierceness.

"Please let her finish." Dr. Markley said with a firm voice.

Keren had become her protector the past few months. And her cheerleader. But Angelina had learned from Dr. Markley that too much protection was as bad as too little. Even though Keren's heart was in the right place, too much protection from Keren had allowed her to get trapped again. Not with Luther, of course, but it still hadn't been good for Angelina to stay in Keren's guest bedroom for months.

If Nate hadn't shown up, who knows how long she'd have been there. Now that she was out of it, she had no intention of getting trapped in it again. "I've spent my life doing nothing. Living off the money I've inherited. Sure, I'm involved in a few charities, but most of my life has been about me. I'm tired of that life. I'm not sure what that means yet, but I...I need to do something. Something that makes a difference. Something important."

"I think that's wonderful, Angelina." Peter smiled. "If there's a way we can help, let us know. We want to support you in any way we can."

"Thanks, Peter."

"Of course. We'll do anything you need. I just meant there's no reason for you to get a job." Keren looked at Dr. Markley. "It's not as if she needs the money.

"Don't you think I'm capable of getting a job?"

"Well...I just...jobs are stressful. Believe me, I know that. People telling you to do this, and that. And do it now. And that's not the right way. Do it again. Very stressful. Don't you agree, Doctor Markley?"

"That's true. Jobs are stressful but—"

"See." Keren looked pleased as if the doctor had agreed with her. "It's not like you need the money, Angelina. Besides you didn't work before. I thought the point of all this was get you back to the way you were. You were fine the way you were."

Angelina wished that were true. Even Luther knew she'd become spoiled and selfish. *Don't think about him.* She shook her head. "I'm not the same person I was. I can never be that person again. And the truth is I don't even want to be that person anymore. I want more in my life than going out partying and spending money. I want to find a way to help people." Angelina looked at the doctor to see what she thought about it.

Dr. Markley nodded with enthusiasm. "That's a wonderful attitude, Angelina. I completely agree with you. Being a contributing member of society is important. And I didn't get to finish what I was about to say. Jobs can be stressful, but not all stress is a bad thing."

"Jobs aren't the answer to everything," Keren said. "They can even be more stressful."

"True but doing a job well can help build self-esteem. When we do a job well, whatever it is, it makes us feel good about ourselves."

"And you think Ange needs more self-esteem?" Keren asked.

"Angelina." Angelina corrected her cousin.

"Sorry, I meant Angelina. Anyway, she's always had more than enough self-esteem."

"I know it might have seemed that way but I'm not sure that was ever true, Keren. I've come to realize I might have been hiding behind the glamorous image of Ange."

The doctor smiled at her.

It had taken a long time for Angelina to admit that during their sessions.

"I'd like you to explain to Keren why you felt the need to change your name," Dr. Markley said. "That way she'll be more understanding about it."

"Mostly because that man...Luther...called that name over and over. Almost like a taunt." She shuddered. "I hate that name now. Plus, Ange was all about herself. I want to be different now. I...I want to be someone my parents would be proud of."

"I'll try to use Angelina from now on. It's just a hard habit to break."

"I know."

"And nothing wrong with changing your name. A lot of people do. But if it's because you're ashamed of what happened to you, that's a different story." The doctor looked up from the notes she'd been writing. "Just remember, Angelina, you've done nothing to be ashamed of."

"I wouldn't say it's about shame. It's more about..." She searched for the right words. "I don't want to sound as if I'm bragging, but I was famous. Maybe not as famous as some people but famous enough. I just want to live a quiet life now. Not be in the media spotlight."

"That sure doesn't sound like you, Angelina. You loved all that hoopla and excitement," Keren said. "I don't think you should give all that up because of Luther Marks."

"I'm a different person. I don't need all that attention." She shrugged. "Besides everyone just wants to feel sorry for me and treat me as if I'm a fragile tea cup about to shatter."

The doctor made another note then looked up. "Maybe that's because you feel that way. Do you? Feel like a fragile tea cup?"

Angelina hadn't thought this would turn into a therapy session. "Not really. I just don't want them to pity me."

"I can understand that. But this isn't about them. It's about you, I don't think you should talk and talk about it all the time to the exclusion of other things. But when the situation calls for it, you need to be able to discuss it. Honestly and openly. Especially with those closest to you." Dr. Markley nodded toward Keren and Peter.

"I don't like talking about it. What's the point? It

won't change what happened."

"True, but talking gets it out of your head." Dr. Markley looked at Keren. "Does she talk about it with you?"

"No." Keren looked at Angelina. "Not really, but you can't blame her. It was a horrible ordeal. I wouldn't want to relieve such a nightmare either. As far as I'm concerned it's in the past and that's where it needs to stay."

Angelina smiled at her cousin, grateful that someone understood. Of course, she thought about it and relived it in her nightmares almost every night. Even daytime was hard, sometimes.

"I don't feel comfortable forcing the issue," Peter said. "But we're here for you, Angelina. You know that. If you want to talk, we'll listen."

"I know that, Peter. You've both been so kind. Letting me live with you. Letting me invade your privacy. It's not fair to you. You're practically newlyweds. You need your privacy."

"We don't mind at all. As Keren always says, family helps family." Peter sounded sincere.

"Which brings us back to the point I want to talk about today. Your living arrangement. It sounds as if you're planning to go back to your cousin's. Is that true?"

Angelina glanced at Dr. Markley. Something in her tone made her think the good doctor disapproved. "I guess. But not forever. Unless you don't think I should go back at all?"

"It's not about what I think." The doctor tapped her index fingers together. "But at some point, you need to live on your own again. And it might be easier if you do it when you leave here. If you go back to their house it will be too easy to fall back into old routines."

Living on her own was just another way of saying being alone. Which was why nobody had even known she was missing. But Dr. Markley was right. She couldn't expect to live with Keren and Peter forever. Her father would be ashamed of her for being weak, depending on others to take care of her. "You're right. It's time I learn to live by myself again."

Keren leaned forward. "I don't think she's ready for that quite yet. But I'm sure you must be so tired of our tiny house. It's nothing like what you're accustomed to." She turned to the doctor. "Angelina has a wonderful home in Mt. Pleasant. Not like our little house."

"You have a lovely home, too." Angelina told her cousin. "And I really do appreciate you letting me live there with you."

"And I love you living there, but, maybe the doctor's right. It might be time to think about other…living arrangements."

"You don't want me to live with you?"

"No, that's not what I meant at all, Angelina. But the doctor says you need to regain your independence. Maybe, you should move back to Mt. Pleasant and Peter and I could live in that apartment above the garage. It's still there, right?"

Angelina didn't want to live in her childhood home. Too many rooms. Too many places for a person to hide. And it represented everything she used to be. Money and extravagance. "That apartment is even smaller than the house you have now."

"But that way we could live right beside each other. You could come over anytime you wanted. Even for dinner every night, but you could still have your independence as well. We wouldn't mind, would we, Peter? If it helps you."

"But it's such a long drive back to Cleveland for Peter's job." Angelina interjected before Peter could answer.

"Not that long." Peter nodded. "And that way we could save the money to buy our own house someday."

"There's no way I'll let the two of you live in that tiny apartment. It barely has the right to be called an apartment, but you could live in the main house. I could live in that apartment. It would be fine for me. I'm only one person."

Keren's eyes widened. "Well, I never thought of that. But if that's what you want, I guess that would be fine with us. Wouldn't it, Peter?"

"Sure. Why not?"

"The house is just sitting there, and I'm paying for the upkeep on it anyway. Of course, I forgot to renew my landscaping contract, but that's been taken care of now. I should have offered it to the two of you in the first place. It was rude of me not to. But it would mean more of a drive for you to get to work, Peter."

He shrugged. "Not so much that it would be a problem."

"Whatever you want, Angelina." Keren smiled. "Besides, it might be nice for you to move back to Mt. Pleasant, don't you think? It's a smaller town, and it's your home."

"I guess."

"Great, we've got the housing arrangements down." The doctor made a few more notes. "And the good news is Mt. Pleasant is much closer for your appointments with me. I'd give it a little time before you go job hunting. In the meantime, maybe some volunteer work. There shouldn't be a lot of stress involved in that."

"That might be fun. Until they find out I'm crazy."

Keren leaned toward her. "You're not crazy. You have PTSD and that's very curable, right, Doctor?"

"It certainly is. With time and some effort on your part. Nothing good ever happens without a little effort." She smiled. "Or a lot."

"You keep saying that, but I don't feel as if I'm getting any better. I'm getting worse."

Dr. Markley looked at Angelina. "It only seems that way. But one thing I'll insist on if I agree to release—"

"If you release me? What does that mean?" Maybe she wouldn't have to leave, after all.

"I misspoke. I meant when I release you. Along with your medication and your continued counseling sessions with me, I insist you join a support group."

A support group? Angelina was sure there were worse things—but she couldn't think of any.

11

Angelina pulled into a parking spot at the church but didn't get out of the car. She really didn't want to be here. Keren was right—what was the point of listening to everyone else's problems? She had enough of her own, and there was no way she wanted to talk about them to a roomful of strangers. Life was hard enough. What was the point of dwelling on the bad things?

But Angelina really did want to be healthy again. So she would go even if only once. She'd survived Luther Marks so she could survive this.

That first night in her apartment—alone—she'd been terrified. Instead of sleeping, she'd spent the night on the sofa staring at the door, waiting for someone to try to break in. But it had gotten better. At least she could sleep now—with all the lights on, but still, it was sleep.

First step to live alone. Second step to go to a support group. So here she was. Looking at her reflection in the rearview mirror, she put on her dark brown, horn-rimmed glasses. They added one more layer of protection against being recognized. Along with the glasses, her hair was back to her natural chestnut brown. And she'd chosen to have a popular wedge cut, getting rid of her trademark long hair.

And just in case the hair color change, the cut, and the glasses weren't enough, she'd given up the flashy clothes as well. Most days she wore jeans and a T-shirt. She hoped people wouldn't automatically know who she was. She wasn't Ange Matthews any longer. But she needed to find out who Angelina Matthews was.

Maybe this group would help.

Taking a deep breath, she opened the car door and walked to the church. Her feet stopped at the door. She really didn't want to go in there. Maybe she'd come next week. Tonight was not the night.

Footsteps pounded on the walk.

Angelina's heart raced, and her fear notched into overdrive.

"Oh, sorry. I didn't mean to startle you, dear." A matronly looking woman, probably in her mid-fifties, stood before her. Her gray hair was pulled back into a ponytail and her hands held two plastic containers.

"Not your fault. I get a little jumpy at noises." Angelina forced a smile.

"Don't we all, dear? You here for the meeting?"

Angelina nodded. "I guess." *Not really.*

"Can you open the door for me?" The woman motioned with her head toward the door. "My hands are full."

Angelina held the door open but didn't move beyond it.

The woman looked back at her. "Come on. It won't be nearly as bad as you think. The first time is always the hardest. But it's been quite helpful to me. I'm sure it can be for you, too."

A picture of her running back to her car flashed in Angelina's mind, but she brushed it away. Time had come to take control of her life. Luther wouldn't win. He'd trapped her in his basement, but that didn't mean she had to stay there. She had to do this.

As Nate said, baby steps.

Of course, this felt more like a giant leap. Angelina took a deep breath and walked inside.

"Don't look so worried, dear. It really isn't as bad as you think." The woman smiled. "My name's Rosie."

"I'm Angelina." She felt like a fraud when she told people her name. She'd gone by the name Ange for so long it was a part of her. A part she wanted to forget.

"What a beautiful name, Angelina. Follow me. I'll show you where the meeting is."

Angelina relaxed as she walked beside Rosie. She'd not given any indication of recognizing her. Maybe no one else would either.

The woman kept up a steady stream of chatter as they walked down one hall and then another. Every now and then Angelina muttered a sound of agreement that seemed to satisfy Rosie since she kept talking.

Surely this woman didn't need a support group. She looked like a grandmother and seemed so normal—even happy. What Angelina wouldn't give to feel that way again.

Eventually they walked into a conference room. A large oval-shaped table dominated the room. It reminded her of the conference room where Dr. Markley had insisted she join a PTSD support group.

There were three people already there—all men. Two sat in chairs, and one was pouring coffee into a ceramic mug.

He turned and smiled as they walked in. "Hey, Rosie. You brought a friend."

"I just met her at the door, but I'm sure she'll become a friend. She looked as if she wanted to run away, but I wouldn't let her." Rosie's laugh tinkled. "It will be good to have another woman here for a change."

"What's that supposed to mean?" One of the men at the table said.

The man with the coffeepot shook his head. "Don't let Rosie make you do anything you don't want to do. We're all about free choice here. You can still run away if you want. The meeting doesn't start for another three minutes. Of course, I hope you'll stay."

Angelina managed a smile, "I'll stay." This time.

He set down his coffee cup down at the head of the table and then shook her hand. "I'm Cooper. These two fellas are Max and Fred."

She glanced in their direction.

A man with a ponytail and a neatly trimmed beard stood and extended his hand. His blue eyes were startling against his tanned complexion and all that hair. "Max."

She leaned over and shook his hand.

Fred gave a wave. "That must mean I'm Fred."

"Angelina."

Fred smiled, but it didn't reach his eyes.

Sadness? Anger? She wasn't sure which.

"And, of course, you already met Rosie." Cooper sat down and took a sip from his mug. "She's been here so long she could run the meeting."

"I wouldn't say that. Then again maybe I could. I feel better when I come so I keep coming." She pointed at the plastic containers. "Besides, who would feed all of you if I didn't show up?" Rosie poured coffee into a cup. "Don't let Cooper kid you. There's nothing unofficial about it. He's Reverend Cooper Stone. He's the preacher here at the church as well as our fearless leader for the group."

"Co-leader. Actually, more like substitute leader. I fill in when the actual leader has to work or can't be here for whatever reason."

"And what's his reason tonight?" Rosie asked. "I miss him when he's gone."

"He's working."

"It figures. He works way too hard." Rosie held a cup out to her. "Want some?"

Angelina shook her head and stared at the table. She'd thought it would be a big enough group that she could blend into the background. She wished she were back in her tiny apartment above the garage.

Max motioned to a chair beside him. "You can sit here. I don't bite. I promise."

She nodded and slid into to her seat, hoping she'd just sink into it and disappear. Her gaze fell on a white board with huge red letters written on it.

'He restoreth my soul.' Psalm 23:3 was written in parentheses.

Cooper must have noticed, because he said, "That's our motto here. No matter what each of us went through, God can and will restore your soul. But that doesn't mean it will be easy."

Psalms? God? A preacher? She'd thought this was a PTSD meeting not a Bible study. Maybe she was in the wrong place. Or she'd come on the wrong night. She wanted to leave, but that would only call more attention to herself.

Cooper stood and walked over to the white board. He wrote: I CAN DO ALL THINGS THROUGH CHRIST WHO STRENGTHENS ME. And in parentheses, Philippians 4:13. That's our verse for this week." Cooper picked up a stack of index cards and passed them to Rosie. Pens followed.

Rosie took one of each and then passed them to Fred, who then looked at Angelina.

"He gives us a Bible verse each week," Rosie explained. "Then we're supposed to meditate on it throughout the week. It really has been most helpful. I read through my stack every day. On a bad day several times. And this is one of my favorites."

"Rosie's our resident optimist," Fred said as he passed the cards to Max. "She loves every verse no matter what it is."

Angelina took the cards and pens from Max. "Thanks."

"You're very welcome."

Definitely a Bible study, not a PTSD group. She found the courage to speak up. "You know I think I'm in the wrong meeting. I wanted the..." She stopped. Could she even say the word aloud? Remembering what Dr. Markley had said about not being ashamed, she finished her sentence. "I wanted the PTSD meeting."

Cooper nodded. "This is the place, sort of. We aren't strictly a PTSD support group but we're all about recovery here. No matter what circumstances brought you. Some probably do have PTSD, whether it's their official diagnosis or not. The point of our group is to support each other as we try to get back to the business of living in a healthy way."

"Oh." Now how was she supposed to get out of here after he said that? "I guess I thought everyone here would have PTSD."

"We may all come from a variety of backgrounds, but our common bond is that our life isn't really working for us the way it should." Cooper's gaze was kind. "But the good news is God promises us beauty for ashes—no matter what caused the ashes in the first place."

As the group wrote the verse, Cooper looked at her. "You did know we were a faith-based group, right?"

"Not really."

"Is that a problem for you?"

Sort of. But when she'd been kidnapped, she'd had no problem praying to God for help. And, miraculously, Nate had shown up out of nowhere. He'd saved her, and then she'd forgotten all about God. Maybe it wouldn't be the worst thing in the world to spend a little time thinking about the Lord. She shrugged. "Not at all."

"For me, God really has been the key to getting healthier. I'm not all the way there, but I'm getting closer," Rosie said.

"Would you like to share how you found our little group? I'm sorry I didn't catch your name the first time." Cooper blew on his coffee and waited for her to respond.

"Angelina."

He nodded. "Angelina, how did you find us, if you don't mind me asking?"

She should have listened to Keren. She was right. This wouldn't help. She didn't want to talk, and she didn't really want to listen to them either. She forced herself to look at Cooper as she answered his question. "My doctor gave me a list of support groups."

"Let me guess, we were the closest to your house," Rosie said as she picked up one of her cookies. "That's how I ended up here, too. Didn't want to drive to a larger city for a support group."

She lifted her gaze to Rosie's. "I hate to admit it,

but that's kind of how I picked this meeting, too."

"Well, nothing wrong with that. But now I come to church here as well. Love the place. Cooper will have to kick me out if they want to get rid of me."

"Why would we want to do that, Rosie? Especially when you bring such delicious cookies." Cooper grinned at Rosie, took a sip of his coffee, and set it on the table. "Seriously though, we're all at different places spiritually. It's not a requirement that you be a Bible-thumper like me to come to the meetings. I hope you'll give us a chance. Come to a few meetings, and if we're not the right group, I'll help you find one that is. Deal?"

She smiled. "Deal."

"Of course, God is a part of this group. Without Him, none of us will really ever be as healthy as we would be with Him. And that's true for everyone whether they've had a trauma in their life or not. We always start and end with a prayer. So let's get started."

Around the table, heads bowed and eyes closed.

Angelina closed hers as Cooper asked for God's healing for each of them. She'd never thought about that before. Could God really do that? For her?

After an amen, Cooper lifted his head. "As I said before, we're all here because there's something in our life that's not working for us." Cooper looked at the group. "Some even to the point that it haunts us so much so that we can't seem to get back into the swing of life."

That certainly was true for her.

"Anyone want to share part of their—"

The door opened and a man walked in. A good-looking man. With a smile, he asked, "Is this where the support group meets?"

Cooper nodded. "You found it."

"Sorry I'm late." He held out his hand to Cooper and shook. "Stephen Smith."

They went through the introductions again.

"We might as well go over our rules for the newcomers. Get yourself a cup of coffee, Stephen, before we start." Cooper smiled and waved a hand toward a chair.

Stephen Smith poured himself a cup then sat down between Angelina and Cooper. He nodded at her with a smile and then looked at Cooper. "OK, let's hear about these rules."

"They're simple. Number one, be respectful. Number two, be honest. Number three, just like they say about Vegas, whatever happens here stays here."

"Only three rules?" Stephen asked.

"I told you they were simple."

Rosie picked up the cookies and passed them to Fred. "Well, they're not as simple as they seem. For example, rule two says be honest, but that doesn't mean you have to answer every question that gets thrown out. If your honest answer is that you don't want to answer, that's OK, too."

Fred picked up a cookie. "And being honest with the group is a cakewalk compared to being honest with yourself. That's the really hard part. At least it has been for me."

Cooper scooted the round cookie container across the table toward Stephen. "Rosie's right. Never feel you have to share more than you're ready to share. But also know, sooner or later, you've got to get out of your comfort zone. Talking about your problem is part of moving forward. And moving forward is part of getting healthy. Getting healthy isn't always easy and it takes a lot of baby steps to get there."

Rosie nodded with enthusiasm. "It's sort of like when I decided to lose weight and get healthy. My first goal was five pounds, and then another five. It wasn't easy, but I lost fifty pounds because I was willing to take that first baby step and try something new."

"And you look beautiful, Rosie," Cooper said. "The new behaviors foster new thinking patterns, but the reverse is true also. New thinking patterns foster new behaviors. They work together. But the good thing is we don't do it all at once. How do we do it, group?"

"Baby steps." They called out at the same time.

That was exactly what Nate had told her, so there must be some truth in it.

"Exactly right. Baby steps. Like the old Chinese proverb that says a journey of a thousand miles begins with the first step. So, as long as you're taking those baby steps, you'll get to your destination eventually."

Max smiled at her. "It's like being in a time warp. It's like our life is a clock and for whatever reason we get stuck in that one moment and can't get out. We're trapped. The clock stops moving. The baby steps start the clock ticking again."

Cooper continued. "Saint Paul urges us to not look behind us but rather to move forward. Of course, that's easier said than done."

Sounded simple enough, but how was she supposed to do that? To move forward when all she could think about was Luther Marks and the things he'd done to her in his basement.

"Who wants to share some of their story with the newcomers?" Cooper reached for a cookie.

"I have this amazing wife and now we have a kid

but...I can't break old habits," Fred started talking. "I really was stuck. When I was a kid, I made some bad choices. Got in trouble with the law. But I thought that was all behind me." Fred fiddled with his pen for a moment. "Then we had our baby. And kids are so expensive. So I fell back to my old habit of looking for quick and easy ways to get rich. Take it from me; get-rich schemes don't work, especially when you get caught. The judge gave me a second chance, and so did my wife. I'm here looking to break the old habits."

"Thanks, Fred. How's that going?"

He shrugged. "Still have my minimum wage job, but I keep looking for something better. But it's not easy when you have a record."

Max looked at her and then at Stephen. "Afghanistan happened to me. And I do have the official PTSD diagnosis, so you're not alone, Angelina. Along with depression." He shrugged and then smiled. "When I came back I moved into my parents' basement and wouldn't leave. They finally had to kick me out and tell me to go find a life. So I'm trying."

That sounded like her in Keren and Peter's guest bedroom.

"Max claims he's a writer but we've yet to read any of his work." Cooper grinned at Max.

Her pulse ramped up. A writer? A writer would probably love to get the inside story of her abduction.

"That's because I'm still in the learning stage. One of these days I'll bring something in for y'all to read."

"That's what you say every time, Max." Rosie took her turn. "I'm a victim...No. I'm a survivor of domestic abuse. You name it and my ex-husband did it to me. I won't lie. It's still difficult for me to talk about, but it's even more difficult to believe I was that stupid to tolerate his abuse. And for so many years."

"You weren't stupid, Rosie. And you didn't tolerate anything. You left." Cooper kept his voice soft but firm. His gaze flicked to Angelina. "That's part of rule one. No name calling. Especially about ourselves."

"Yeah, but it took a lot longer than it should have." Rosie shook her head. "I still have trouble believing just what I tolerated."

"Things take as long as they take. Real life isn't on a timeline." Cooper smiled at Rosie, and then looked back at her. "In a way if we've had a trauma in our life, we probably have a form of PTSD. And that means we probably keep reliving the incident over and over. That's the getting trapped part that Fred talked about."

"It's not just thinking about it." Max's fingers tapped on the table as he talked. "But you actually relive it. You can smell it, hear the noises. Practically reach out and touch the guy next to you."

He was so right about that. She could still hear Luther's footsteps and feel his breathing on her neck. Not to mention the stabbing pain when he'd poked her with one of his knives. In the dark.

She hadn't slept in the dark since then.

"The thing is, you've got to find a way to make the clock start ticking again so you can move out of that moment. Until you do that, you can't move forward. Can't get healthy." Cooper's smile encompassed the whole group. The man smiled a lot, but he was good at putting people at ease.

Rosie reached for the second plastic container she'd brought with her. "Anyone want another cookie?" she asked as she opened it. She handed the container to Fred.

He took it. "Rosie believes that cookies will help in

any situation." He took two cookies and passed the container to Max. "I'm starting to believe she might be right. At least about her cookies."

"So, how do you move forward?" Stephen asked.

She was relieved he'd asked the question. She was afraid to speak up. It seemed like an impossible task to move forward. It had been months ago, but it still felt as if it had happened yesterday. Fear ruled her life.

"There's no one right way to do it. I'm still in the process of figuring that one out, too." Rosie took a deep breath. "Time helps. But it's bizarre. Anything can send me right back to my ex-husband. Even a word. Then I feel my panic rising. Knowing I'll get hit any moment. Or worse."

Max leaned around Stephen so he could see her. "Don't let whatever happened to you in the past steal your future from you. I almost let that happen. In my parents' basement. Good thing they got tired of me, or I'd still be there."

It was the same thing Nate had told her. They were both right. That's exactly what she'd been doing. Letting Luther Marks steal her future. Her peace. Her joy. Her life. She wanted to start her clock ticking again. She was so tired of being in that basement with Luther.

"And just so you and Stephen know, there's no pressure to tell your story. You'll know when the time is right." Cooper told them.

"Oh, I don't mind," Stephen spoke up. He spent the next fifteen minutes telling how he'd been robbed at gunpoint and now he couldn't sleep. And since he couldn't sleep it was beginning to affect his job. His doctor had told him about this meeting so he was giving it a try. When he finished Stephen looked at

Angelina. "What about you? What brought you here?"

"This is her first night as well." Cooper touched her arm. "No pressure. Do you want to talk about it, Angelina?"

She shook her head. "Not yet." Not ever.

"Any other suggestions to help Angelina and Stephen get started with breaking that cycle of reliving the traumatic event?"

"The first one seems obvious. If you know something triggers the memories than stay away from it," Rosie said. "That's why I never, ever make coconut macaroons. And probably never will. My ex-husband's favorite. Just smelling coconut makes me sick to my stomach."

"Makes sense," Angelina replied.

"Get out of your comfort zone. Do completely new things. Go to new places, eat new foods. Force yourself to enjoy life. Make new memories." Fred told them. "Even if it kills you."

"Well, not if it kills you, Fred. That's a bit of an exaggeration." Rosie nodded her agreement. "But it is important to stay busy. But not busy for busyness's sake. Do something that is important. Something that will make the world a better place."

That was the way Angelina had been raised. Both her parents had drummed that philosophy into her. They'd told her over and over, 'With great blessings come great responsibilities.'

Of course, she hadn't done that. Instead, she'd partied and made herself the center of attention. But that would change. She was done with that life. She wanted to help other people—in some small way.

Rosie pointed at her cookies that were almost gone. "I know it sounds corny, but I believe God created each of us to do good things for other people. I bake not just for these guys, but I take cookies and cupcakes to a different nursing home in the area every week."

"That sounded depressing," Stephen said.

"It's not at all depressing. The residents love getting some company along with a home-made cookie. I make their day a little brighter and that makes me a bit happier."

Cooper nodded. "Rosie's absolutely right. Thinking about someone other than yourself will do wonders. And volunteering is a great way to do that."

Dr. Markley had encouraged her to do that, too. She just wasn't sure how to get started. Now that she was back in Mt. Pleasant, there might not be a lot of opportunities.

"So, we always like to take a minute to share how our week went. A victory and a struggle. That way the struggle can become a new goal for you. And the victory celebrates our baby steps of success." Cooper looked at the group. "Who wants to go first?"

Rosie raised her hand. "It's not really a big deal, but I didn't vacuum my carpet today." She looked over at Angelina. "My husband had a strict rule that I had to vacuum every day. I realized last week I was still doing it. Not because the carpet needed cleaned but out of habit. So I stopped."

"Good for you, Rosie." Cooper gave her a thumbs-up. "Celebrate the victories no matter how small they may seem. Each victory moves us a step forward. For Angelina and Stephen, coming to the meeting was a great victory. And we applaud you for that decision."

They clapped, and Fred even threw in a yahoo.

"So coming here was your victory. What was your

struggle, Angelina?"

"Coming here." Angelina smiled.

Cooper laughed. "There you have it. So your goal for next week is to come back to the meeting. Think you can handle it?"

"Well, I did it tonight, so I think I can do it again next week."

Rosie patted her arm. "Good attitude."

After they each shared a victory and a struggle, the group ended with a prayer.

She was at her car when she heard footsteps approaching. Her pulse ramped up.

"Hey, Angelina." Cooper stopped several feet from her. "I just wanted to thank you for staying for the meeting even though it's not what you were expecting. If you give it time, it will help. I promise."

"I was afraid it would be a sermon or something."

"Not at all. But God should be a part of every area of our lives. Especially our healing. I have regular office hours here at the church. Feel free to drop in during the week if you need some extra support. Or if you'd like to talk about your relationship with God."

A relationship with God? What did that even mean? "Thanks." After Cooper walked away, she slid into her seat. She was just about to put her car in gear when someone knocked on the window.

Stephen Smith. The other newcomer.

She rolled the window down. "Hey, Angelina. I thought you might want to grab a cup of coffee with me. Seems as if we have a lot in common."

"I'm sorry. I really can't."

He looked disappointed. "OK, maybe another time."

She drove off.

12

"I made muffins this morning." Keren stood at Angelina's door with a bowl. She waved it under her nose. "They didn't turn out half-bad for a first effort. Banana walnut."

"They smell great."

"Got some coffee to go with them?"

"Not yet, but I can make some."

"I'm liking this not working thing. Of course, I'll start looking for a job. Soon. I have no plans to live off your generosity. But not quite yet." Keren smiled.

"Don't find a job on my account. If you don't want to work, it doesn't matter to me." Angelina walked over to the small kitchenette area.

"You shouldn't be living in this tiny place. It's just not right. I really feel bad. Why don't you move in with us? There's more than enough room."

"I'm fine here, Keren. And I've imposed on you and Peter long enough."

"Imposed? We're the ones living in your house. Which I might add is an amazing house. I can't believe how big it is. You were much too kind to let us live there when you're the one who should be. Instead of living in this glorified attic."

Angelina held up a box with assorted coffee containers. "What's your poison? French vanilla. Mocha caramel. Or just plain old black?"

"French vanilla for me."

Angelina picked a package out of the box and placed it in the gourmet coffeemaker. She'd given up a lot when she'd moved in here, but she wasn't giving up her coffeemaker. She placed a cup under the machine and then found another cup for herself. "I think I'll have mocha caramel." A few moments later, she handed the coffee-filled mug to Keren. "The truth is I like it here. Don't ask me why, but I feel safe. Nobody can sneak in without me knowing it. There's only one door in and out. And since it's above the garage, they can't just crawl in through a window."

"Well, if you say so. But whenever you're ready to move back into your house, let us know. It's not like there isn't room enough for all of us. So how was your meeting last night? Probably pretty lame, right?"

"It was OK. The people seemed nice." Angelina picked up her mocha caramel and walked to a chair.

Keren followed behind with her own cup.

Angelina tore off a bite of the muffin and popped it in her mouth. She grinned and gave a thumbs-up as flavor burst on her tongue.

Keren rolled her eyes. "Nice? They were probably losers."

"Yeah, losers like me." She sipped her coffee. Perfect.

Keren's face reddened. "I didn't mean it like that. You're not a loser. You have a right to...well, you know what I mean. You went through so much. It's all right if it's taking you some time to adjust."

"One thing I learned last night is that I'm not the only person in the world to whom bad things have happened. Bad things happen to lots of people and they survive." She swallowed another bite of her muffin. "Maybe I can, too."

"Of course, you will, sweetie. I know you will."

"It turned out to be a faith-based group."

"What's that mean?"

"The preacher is one of the leaders of the group. He says God wants to be part of everything in our lives, especially our healing."

Keren shrugged. "So now that you've kept your promise, I guess you don't have to go back any more."

"It's not like I have a whole lot else to do. I'll probably go a few more times. It can't hurt. And who knows? It might actually help."

"I sure wouldn't want to have to talk to a room full of strangers about..." Keren shuddered. "About all the horrible things that man did to you."

"It's not like that. I don't have to talk about anything if I don't want. It's more about encouraging us to not give up on living."

"I guess that's all fine and dandy. It just seems like a waste of time to me."

"Well, I have plenty of time to waste. That's for sure."

"Well, I don't. That house is so huge, and it takes me forever to clean it, so I've got to get going or I won't be done in time for dinner."

"Oh, Keren, I'm so sorry. You're right. It is too big for one person to clean. I'll call the cleaning company today to help you out."

"That's not what I meant. I wasn't complaining at all. I love living there."

"I know. Will two mornings a week be enough?"

"More than enough. You're just too nice to me. So what are your plans for the day?"

"Not much. Maybe I'll take a drive later."

"A drive? That doesn't sound like you."

"Gotta start doing things differently if I want a different sort of life." Baby steps.

~*~

Angelina sat in her car, not quite believing she was here. What had she been thinking? Of all the places to end up when she'd decided to drive around. She should go home. On the other hand, she was here, so she might as well go in. She stepped out of her car and walked up to the church for the second time in two days. Her heart pounded as she knocked on the office door marked with Cooper Stone's name.

A moment later, the door opened. Cooper's eyes widened, but then he smiled. "Angelina. What a wonderful surprise. Please, come in."

"I don't want to be a bother. If you're busy..."

"Not busy at all." He opened the door wider. "Want something to drink? Coffee or water. I might be able to scare up a soda if you like."

"No, thanks."

"Please sit down." He motioned toward a chair.

Instead of walking to the chair behind his desk, he sat down in the other one near her. "So, how are you today? Still processing the meeting?"

"A little. It was a lot to take in. But I'm glad I came. I guess."

"I'm glad you did, too. Life can be really hard. It's always good to have other people in your corner rooting you on."

"I was wond...you talked about..." She smiled. "I'm not really sure why I even came today."

He folded his hands on his lap. "Take all the time you need to spit it out."

"I guess you're not making it easy for me."

He shook his head. "Not my job."

"It's been a long time since I went to church. Actually, since my parents died. But I believe in God. I consider myself a Christian, I suppose. My parents were very involved in our church."

"How did they die?"

"Plane crash. At the same time."

"I'm so sorry. That must have been awful for you."

"It was. I was sixteen at the time. I just sort of started to take care of myself at that point. Kept going to school and stuff."

"That's impressive. So they were very involved in church before that. And yet you stopped going after they died. Why is that?"

"I don't know."

He nodded. "During a tragedy, we either turn to God for support or turn away from him in anger. Would you agree with that?"

She nodded. "I never thought about it like that consciously. It was more a case of thinking, why bother. I had more important things to worry about than going to church. More important things to do."

"But now, you're thinking God might be the answer to your problems."

"Maybe. All I know is that I'm just so tired of my life." She rolled her eyes. "Who am I kidding? I don't really have a life anymore."

"What do you mean?"

"I don't do anything. I don't go places. I don't work. I don't have a life. I don't visit with friends." She paused. "To tell the truth, I don't think I even have any friends. Anymore. Not real ones. A few called after…after…after my incident. But they stopped when I didn't return their calls."

"That probably hurt you."

She shrugged. "They're busy. And I've changed a lot so it's OK. I don't think I have a lot in common with them anymore."

He lifted up his Bible. "Ever hear about sowing and reaping?"

"Maybe." She smiled. "Not really."

"Sowing and reaping is one of God's most important principles. Anyone can change their life at any time, if they start sowing different seeds than what they've been doing."

"What do you mean?"

"Think of our actions as seeds. If we sow selfish seeds, then we get more selfishness in our life. From ourselves and from others. But if we sow seeds of kindness, then we start reaping that kindness as well."

"Sort of like doing good will to all?"

He nodded. "Galatians six nine says, 'Let us not become weary in doing good for at the proper time we will reap a harvest if we do not give up.' I think it's time for you to do some sowing. But know that sowing always brings a harvest. In God's time."

"Any ideas how I'm supposed to do that?"

He grinned again. "Indeed, I do." He pulled out several sheets of papers stapled together. "Here's a list of volunteer programs in the area. Most of them are always in need of people. Look them over and pick one. But my advice is to do it today. Tomorrow you'll find an excuse to put it off until later. And then another excuse and another."

13

Angelina's heels clicked on the faded black and white checked linoleum as she made her way down to the classroom she'd been assigned. Now that she was here, she was regretting her impulsivity. What had she been thinking?

Room 207.

Her hand moved up to the knob but didn't actually connect with the door. Her gaze flitted up and down the hall. No one was around. She could turn and leave.

Go back to her car and go home. The only place she felt relatively safe. It had come as a surprise to her, but the tiny apartment over the garage actually did feel safe. Almost as safe as the clinic.

The garage apartment had been built to house the down-on-their-luck employees their parents hired. Over the years, the apartment had been shelter to a few chauffeurs, a gardener, even a maid. Her family believed in helping others since they'd been blessed more than most.

Another reason why she'd picked this volunteer program from the list Cooper gave her. Their purpose was to read to children who might not get read to at home. The goal was to instill a love of reading and, therefore, create a reader.

Help others less fortunate than herself. It had been her family's mantra.

She'd forgotten it and certainly hadn't been living it.

Cooper was right.

It was time to stop focusing on herself and help someone else for a change.

She stared at the classroom door. But maybe not quite yet. She'd call the school later and make some excuse up about why she couldn't follow through on the volunteer program right now. *Chicken. You're just a chicken.*

She took a deep breath and knocked.

The door opened. The teacher was all smiles. "Good morning. You must be Angelina. I'm Deb, or Miss Dawkins to the children." She leaned closer. "I saw you standing out there and thought you might be having second thoughts. Glad you decided to come in."

"Last minute jitters."

"No reason to have them. The kids will love you." She put a hand on Angelina's arm and guided her to the front of the class. "Class, this is Miss Angelina. She's here to have some fun with us. She'll be reading some great stories with you."

The kids clapped.

Angelina's anxiety level dropped a notch or two. This might not be so bad after all.

"OK, who wants to be in Miss Angelina's reading group today?"

Every child raised their hand except one little boy. He simply stared down at his desk.

"Break into your groups as usual. Miss Angelina will pick three of you to sit with her in the reading corner." Miss Dawkins pointed at the far corner of the room where a bean bag chair sat. A big bright red and yellow sign announced it was the READING CORNER.

The students picked up chairs and formed circles. Each group had five to six children in it. As they seated themselves, they gave her hopeful looks. A few even pointed at themselves trying to get her to pick them.

Angelina chose a beautiful little African-American girl with braids all over her head. Then she picked a boy who couldn't sit still, and finally she went over and touched the shoulder of the little boy who hadn't raised his hand.

The other kids moaned.

"Don't worry. She's coming in twice a week. Everyone will get their turn sooner or later." Deb winked at her and then mouthed, 'they love you.'

Angelina's little group made their way to the back of the room. The little girl took a dive and landed in the bean bag chair. The two boys picked up their own pillows and made themselves comfortable.

What was she supposed to do now?

"Now, I wonder where I'm supposed to sit," she mused aloud.

"You can sit here with me." The girl scooted over.

"That sounds like a wonderful idea, but I'd better find a book first." She looked over at the sad little boy. "What's your favorite book?"

He shook his head.

Her gaze moved to the other boy. "What about you?"

He jumped up and ran to the bookshelf. A moment later, he handed her a book. "*Where the Wild Things Are*. OK, I've never read this one. It looks scary."

"It's not scary." The little girl declared. "Well, not

too scary. Just a little."

Angelina sat in the bean bag chair.

The little girl smiled, obviously happy Angelina had chosen to sit with her.

"Before we get started, tell me your names."

The girl poked Angelina in the arm. "My name is Latasha."

"Nice to meet you. I love your braids."

Latasha's smile grew even bigger as her dark brown eyes sparkled.

Angelina pointed at the boy on the right side of the bean bag. "And yours?"

"I'm Robert English the Third, but everybody calls me Bobby." He pointed at the other boy. "This is Charles. He doesn't like to talk very much."

Angelina smiled at Charles. "Is that right? You don't like to talk?"

He stared down at his lap, not responding to her.

She leaned forward. "That's OK. You don't have to talk to me if you don't want to. But can you shake my hand so I know you're happy to meet me."

After a long moment, he reached his hand toward her.

Afterwards, Angelina walked down the hall with a smile. That was the most fun she'd had in a long time. There might just be something to this sowing and reaping thing Cooper had talked about. She smiled at the policeman walking toward her.

He stopped and stared. "Angelina?"

She stopped and stared. "Nate. I'm so sorry I didn't recognize you in your uniform. And I wasn't really paying attention."

"Don't worry about it. I almost didn't recognize you either. You look great."

"Yeah, I didn't look so great the last time you saw me." She gave a half-smile.

His face flushed. "That's not what I meant. You just...look different. I think you changed your hair or something."

She touched the short wedge cut that was now back to her natural brown. "Yea, blonde was Ange. This is Angelina's hair color."

"I like it. It looks great on you. How are you?"

"Fine." The response seemed automatic.

"I've been thinking about you but wasn't sure if I should call or not."

She wouldn't admit she'd wanted him to call. "That's OK."

"So when did you get out of the clinic?"

"Last week. Dr. Markley said I needed to live alone so I moved home."

"That's good. So you're feeling better? Dr. Markley helped?"

"A little, I guess. It's been difficult. Really difficult. Dr. Markley assures me it won't always be that way."

"I'm not surprised after all you've been through." He checked his watch. "I have a little time before I have to get back to work. Why don't we go get a cup of coffee? And maybe a doughnut?"

"A doughnut?"

He patted his stomach and grinned. "What can I say? There's always a little truth in every stereotype. And, really, who doesn't love a doughnut now and then? My car is here. Why don't you follow me in your vehicle?"

"I know I do." As Angelina followed Nate to the little bakery, she berated herself for accepting his invitation. What had she been thinking? What would they even talk about? But he had taken a bullet for her. Saved her life. And if that wasn't enough, he'd be kind enough to find Dr. Markley and her clinic. She really did owe him. The least she could do was have a cup of coffee with the man.

As Cooper said, start sowing seeds of kindness.

In the parking lot, Nate rushed around and opened her car door before she could. He smiled down at her. "I really can't believe how good you look. That hair style is perfect for the new you. And I love the glasses."

She touched her hair, feeling pleased that he liked it. "Thanks. The glasses are fake."

"Fake? Why are you wearing them?"

"I thought they'd keep people from recognizing me."

His smile was compassionate. "They work, because I almost walked right past you."

She went through the door he opened.

They walked up to the counter, ordered their doughnuts and coffee, and then found a booth by a window. Once they had their order, Nate looked at her. "I wanted to check on you after you went to the clinic but I figured I'd give you some time. So how are you? Really?"

She stared at him, wondering if she should speak from her heart or just say the right words everyone wanted to hear. "It's not really been that bad. I was being a bit of a dram—"

"Don't even go there, Angelina. I didn't invite you here so you could tell me what I want to hear. I want to know about you. What's really going on?"

"PTSD." She forced herself to look up from the doughnut. "At least that's what the doctors called it."

"That can be really tough."

"You were right. I'd let Keren's bedroom become another prison. But I'm working really hard to not let that happen again. I'm living back here, but Keren and Peter came along for some support."

"Good for you. Sounds as if you're taking the right steps."

She was pleased that he was pleased. "That's why I was at the school. Volunteering. Trying to think about someone other than myself."

"That's wonderful."

"What about you? Why were you at the school?"

"Same reason. I go read to a different class every week." He touched the shoulders of his uniform. "Always in my uniform. I want the kids to learn to trust policemen, not to be afraid of us."

"That's so nice."

He winked. "Not all that nice. It really is fun for me. I enjoy the kids."

"Yeah, I have to admit I had a good time today, too. The kids were so excited to have me there. I can't remember the last time somebody was that happy to see me."

"The Bible says unless you become like little children, you will never enter the kingdom of heaven. So spending some time with kids seems like a good idea. Keeps me grounded. I can learn from them."

"I don't know many people like you."

"What do you mean?"

"You're always talking about God and the Bible. It must be a big part of your life."

"It is. And I'm proud of it. How about you? Are you a Christian?"

"Yeah, I guess so. I mean I'm not really sure. It's

been a long time since I went to church or anything."

He set his coffee cup down. "We should do something about that. How about church with me this Sunday?"

Church? She wasn't quite ready for that yet, but maybe one day. "I...uh...I don't think so."

"No problem. If you change your mind, let me know." He looked over at the counter. "I think I need one more of those chocolate doughnuts. How about you?"

She shook her head. "I better pass."

He seemed so nice. So real. Genuine. Not like Zarlengo or any of her celebrity friends. Still she probably should call Zarlengo to let him know she was OK, and that she didn't harbor any hard feelings. While she was at it, she should call back some of her other friends who'd called to check on her after...after Luther Marks.

When he was back with the doughnut, he sat down. "I'll need to run an extra mile today."

"Do you run?"

"Gotta stay fit in this job so I run a few times a week and go to the gym a couple of times as well." He looked at her thoughtfully. "That might be a good idea for you."

"You think I'm fat?"

"Not in the least, and you know it. If you're fishing for a compliment, I'll give it to you. You look terrific. He laughed. "But physical exercise is good for the soul as well as for the body."

"I wasn't fishing for anything."

He winked. "Sure you weren't."

~*~

When she pulled into the drive, Keren rushed out to her car.

Angelina pulled into the six-car garage and stepped out.

"Where have you been?" Keren was breathless. "I was about to call out the National Guard to look for you. I've been worried to death."

"I'm so sorry, Keren. I didn't mean to worry you. I told you I might take a drive."

"But I didn't know it would be for that long. You've been gone for hours and hours. Where'd you go?" Keren demanded. Her voice had a note of fear.

It suddenly occurred to Angelina that her initial disappearance had affected Keren more strongly than she'd thought. Her cousin did love her, and the trauma of possibly losing someone was evident in her tone, despite the aggressiveness. Angelina tucked that thought away to examine later. "Certainly not where I expected. I ended up going to the elementary school and reading to some first graders."

"You did what?"

Angelina explained her visit with Cooper and then the school.

Keren visibly relaxed and smiled as she listened. "Well, that sounds wonderful. It really does. Just make sure you don't try to do too much too soon. You don't want to get...umm...relive terrible things again."

"And then I went out for coffee."

"By yourself?"

"With a friend actually." Angelina smiled. It felt good to say that.

"And who was that?"

Keren's mother-hen attitude was a bit surprising to Angelina, who'd not really answered to anyone since her parents passed away. She'd need to talk with Keren about that sooner or later. Later was better. "I ran into Nate Goodman at the school. We went out for coffee and doughnuts."

"Nate Goodman? He keeps popping up. Are you sure he's not stalking you?"

Angelina's heart rate jumped. "What an awful thing to say. He's been so kind to me."

"You're right. I'm so sorry." Keren looked ready to cry. "Blame it on me being worried. But why would you want to go anywhere with him? He's just a cop."

"Why not? And he asked me to go to church with him on Sunday."

"Church?" Keren squeaked. "Are you going?"

"I might one of these days. He really is cute. And Nice. And so easy to talk to. But no, I told him I wasn't ready to go to such a public place yet."

"Can't blame you for that. Besides how many people even go to church these days?"

"I have no idea. But I might check it out."

Keren's eyes widened. "Really? What could church possibly do for you?"

That was a good question. One Angelina hoped to find an answer to—soon.

14

"I went out on a date this week," Rosie announced to the group as she set two containers of cookies in front of them. "Chocolate chip. And this other one is raisins and white chocolate."

"I can't tell you how happy I am that you find baking therapeutic, Rosie dear." With one hand Max reached for a chocolate chip and with the other, reached for the raisin cookie.

Angelina had come for this third meeting, and she was feeling slightly more comfortable. Everyone was so kind. So understanding. No one tried to tell her what she should or shouldn't feel.

Stephen picked up a cookie. "Wow. That's real progress, Rosie. I remember when you said you'd never marry, let alone date again. So how'd it go?"

"Oh, not well. Not well at all, I'm afraid." She frowned. "But I went out on the date, so that's a victory in itself, right? Even if I didn't have fun."

Curiosity got the better of Angelina. "Why didn't you have fun? What happened?"

"Well, everything was fine at first. He took me to a nice restaurant in Canton and then…" Rosie sat down as she gave a dramatic pause. "Then the waitress brought over the menus. And that's when things started to go downhill."

"Why?"

"When she handed me a menu, my date snatched

it out of my hand and gave it back to her. He told her that he would order for me." She grabbed a chocolate chip cookie. "Now, keep in mind we barely know each other and he has no idea what I like or don't like."

"What did you do?" Fred asked as he picked up a few cookies.

"I very politely told him that I was a picky eater and wanted to look at the menu. He gave me a look and said that was a surprise, and then went on to say that he assumed I liked to eat most anything."

"Oh, no. How awful," Angelina said. She'd had a few dates like that.

"What's wrong with that?" Fred asked before he stuffed the whole cookie in his mouth.

"Men." Rosie rolled her eyes and looked at Angelina. "You get it, don't you?"

Angelina nodded. "Oh, I get it. So what did you do?"

"Well...I looked at him for a moment. Then I said, 'you're right.' I do like to eat most anything, but I'm very picky about who I eat it with. Then I got up and marched out of the restaurant."

"Way to go, Rosie. Don't you let that man put you down like that. We love you just the way you are. Wouldn't change a thing about you," Max said between bites. "How'd you get home if you were in Canton?"

"Called a taxi."

Angelina thought about that moment when she'd chosen to walk over to Luther's limo instead of waiting for a taxi. She shuddered. She didn't think she'd ever be able to take a limo or a taxi again. Heat washed over her, and the air turned close, stuffy. She wasn't sure if she'd be able to find her next breath.

Rosie pointed at Angelina. "Do you think I was being too sensitive?"

Don't think about it. Angelina struggled to take a deep breath without anyone noticing and shook her head so they'd not notice her distress. "Not at all, Rosie." *Luther can't hurt me anymore.*

Fred looked over at Rosie. "I still don't get what was so bad."

Stephen shook his head. "Fred, he was telling her she was fat. That she ate too much."

"Ohhh…that wasn't nice. At all." Fred smiled. "I don't think you're fat. I think you're just right."

"Thanks, Fred. But you're way too young for me." Rosie's laugh tinkled through the room.

"My wife wouldn't like that anyway. But Max is a bachelor. What about you, Stephen? Are you married?"

"Divorced."

"You weren't being too sensitive, Rosie. He was just downright rude." Angelina took a nibble of the chocolate chip. "You should start a bakery."

"That's good to know. I wasn't sure. Not about the bakery. About my date. But maybe a bakery is a good idea, too."

The door opened.

Nate Goodman walked in.

What was he doing here?

He looked at her, seeming to be as surprised as she was. But then he looked away. "Sorry I'm late. What did I miss?"

"Oh, not much. Just Rosie telling us how she put her date in his place," Fred said. "I don't know exactly why, but everyone else seems to think it was the right thing to do."

Max laughed. "You are clueless, buddy. Clueless. How did you ever get a woman to date you, let alone marry you?"

Nate smiled, but his eyes were still focused on her. "I see we have some newcomers since the last time I was here. I'm Nate. Cooper and I take turns with the meetings."

Nate was the leader of the meeting? No wonder he kept saying the same things. Now it made sense. Nate turned to Rosie. "So you went on a date. That's awesome."

"But it didn't go well."

"Why?"

"Angelina says it was his fault," Fred said as he reached for another cookie.

"That's good enough for me. Who's Angelina?" He gave her a questioning glance.

Angelina hid her smile, thankful Nate hadn't outed her in front of the group. On the other hand, Dr. Markley had told her she had nothing to be ashamed of.

And Nate was the hero of her story. He shouldn't have to hide that fact from the group. It seemed dishonest. She took a deep breath. "It's OK, Nate. They might as well know the truth."

Nate's expression went from surprise to proud.

She'd done the right thing. That made her feel good as if she'd accomplished something important.

"What truth?" Fred asked.

She stared, not ready to tell them the whole story yet.

Nate stepped in. "Angelina and I have had a few dealings with each other before."

"Oooh," Fred said. "I know what that means. I've

been on the wrong side of the law way too many times myself. But no more."

"It wasn't like that, Fred," Nate replied. "So Angelina says it wasn't your fault, Rosie."

"That's what she says. And I believe her." Rosie explained the situation to Nate.

"So that wasn't just a baby step, Rosie. That was a huge step. And even more huge that you recognized he wasn't right for you, and that you didn't let him get away with being rude. I'm very proud of you."

"That's true. I did that."

"Anybody else take any baby steps they'd like to share?"

"I started volunteering at a school." Angelina smiled at the group. "Cooper told us we should start thinking about other people, not just our problems."

Nate smiled. "Wonderful idea."

"Well, I'm not doing all that much. I just read them a book and talk to them a little bit."

After a prayer, he passed out the index cards to write the verse of the week. "Isaiah 28:10: 'For it is precept upon precept, line upon line, here a little, there a little'. Anybody want to tell me what they think this means?"

Stephen spoke up. "I guess it's saying nothing happens instantly. We learn a little, then a little more, and then a little more. One step at a time. Or as you'll say, baby steps."

Cooper nodded. "Exactly. Rome wasn't built in a day, and we won't get healthy in a day. One day at a time. Just like Rosie going out on her first date and Angelina volunteering. One step forward can get that clock unstuck and moving in the right direction again. And as Rosie proved, it doesn't have to be perfect to be progress."

"Good to know," Fred said. "My wife's talking about letting me move back in. But only in the guest room. She's says she's proud that I've kept this job for two months. But it's such a nowhere job."

"Moving back in is an amazing step. One step at a time. She probably wants to see if she can trust you or not."

"Oh, she can. I'm done with drinking and get-rich schemes. All I want is a good job that lets me take care of my family the way they deserve."

Before she even realized what she was doing, Angelina spoke up. "Speaking of jobs, I heard that they're hiring at Diamond. You should put in an application, Fred. That's a good place to work, isn't it?"

"Sure I'd love to work there, but chances are they won't hire a guy with my record."

She made a mental note to call the plant manager first thing in the morning. "You never know. They might. At least put in an application. It's worth a shot."

"Fine, I will."

She smiled, pleased that she could really help someone and make a difference. It was a good feeling.

The discussion continued.

As the group was about to break up, Angelina found her courage. "I... I...uh...thought it was time to tell the group what happened. To me."

"Only if you're ready, Angelina. We don't want you to tell us until you're ready. There's no pressure here. Ever."

"I'm ready."

"OK, take your time."

Fred pointed at the container. "And a cookie. They help."

With a forced smile, she picked up a cookie. A sigh escaped. "I...I don't even know how to begin. I told myself I'd tell the group what happened tonight. But I didn't actually think about what I'd say." She snapped the cookie in two. "I guess I should have thought about that."

"You don't have to tell us, Angelina." Rosie put a protective arm around her. "It's OK."

Tears filled Angelina's eyes. "No, I want to tell." But after she did, they wouldn't look at her the same. Keren and Peter still handled her differently. Still, she wanted to get better, and this was part of the process. "I need to tell you. I...I..." Her voice dropped off.

This was harder than she'd expected. She crammed the cookie in her mouth to buy time. After she ate it and before she could change her mind, she blurted out the story. "I guess maybe the easiest way to tell you is to tell you the name I used to go by. Until a few months ago, I used the name Ange Matthews."

Nobody said anything for a moment.

"You mean that Ange Matthews." Stephen broke the silence. "The woman who was kidnapped?"

She dared to look up.

They all stared at her with a mixture of expressions. Shock, surprise, compassion, and even sadness, painted their faces.

Rosie looked at her, then at Nate. "Oh, my," Rosie said as she made the connection between the two of them. Then she pushed the chocolate chip cookie plate toward her. "Have another cookie, dear."

"Yeah, I'm sure a chocolate chip cookie will make her feel better." Max chuckled. "Not."

The others laughed, and before she knew it, she was laughing as well.

After a minute or so, Nate shook his head. "Well, that was certainly one of the strangest stories we've had."

"I didn't mean for it to come out quite like that."

Rosie patted her arm and then grabbed a couple of cookies. "What a nightmare that must have been. But you're safe now, and you're in the process of healing, so that's good."

"Angelina and Stephen, everyone else has my phone number and I want you both to have it as well. If you need me for anything feel free to call." After he gave them the number, he had each of them call him so their numbers would be in his phone. "Feel free to call anytime, day or not. I'm used to being called in the middle of the night, so it's not a problem."

As she walked to her car, Stephen jogged up beside her. "I'm glad you shared your story with us, Ange."

"My name is Angelina. Not Ange."

He touched her arm. "Sorry, I just shortened it. I didn't mean to offend you."

She fought the urge to shake it away. "No problem. I want to be called Angelina now."

"All right, Angelina. Anyway, I'm glad you were able to open up tonight. It's a first step in healing. Or at least that's what everyone says."

What difference did it make to him? *Stop being paranoid.* The guy was just being friendly. He wasn't a stalker. Or was he? His first night at the meeting was the same night as hers. Coincidence? Or something more sinister?

"I was thinking we could go out for some coffee, maybe a late dinner. What do you say?"

"That's nice, but I don't think so." She managed to

say even though she could barely breathe. "I'm not dating right now." She stood in front of her car, but he didn't move away. She fumbled with her keys, her mind fogged over. Panic seeped in.

"Angelina, are you OK? What's wrong?" Stephen moved closer.

She wanted to push him away. Far away. She leaned against the car, gasping for air. "I...I...I..."

"Just breathe. Hey, Nate. Need a little help over here," Stephen called out.

Her knees no longer held her up, and she slid to the ground.

"Angelina. It's OK." She heard Nate but couldn't speak.

A moment later, Rosie was sitting beside her, rubbing her back.

Nate kept talking. "Angelina, look at me. Look at me. You're safe. Nobody will hurt you."

She turned toward him, still not able to find her voice. She grabbed Rosie's hand.

Rosie smiled at her. "Good girl. You're safe. You're here with us. We won't let anyone hurt you. Take a deep breath and then hold it for a moment."

It was hard to do but Angelina managed. Then another and another. Finally, her world came back into focus.

Rosie was still sitting beside her, Nate sat on the other side, and Max stood in front. Stephen and Fred were behind him. The whole group had formed a protective cocoon around her.

The reality of what had just happened hit her. She was mortified. "Oh, I am so—"

"Don't you say sorry, Angelina." Rosie squeezed her hand. "We're just so glad we were here to keep you safe. There's nothing to be embarrassed about at all. We've all done it at one time or another."

"Yeah, we've all been there." Max told her. "You should have seen me the first night I slept in my own apartment. All I wanted was to be back in my parents' basement."

"Did I do something…say something wrong?" Stephen stepped forward.

She shook her head. "Not really."

"Not really sounds like a yes to me. What did I say?"

Angelina put a hand to her head. "Nothing."

Stephen knelt down by her. "Come on, Angelina. You need to be real about this. It's the only way to getting healthy."

She was so embarrassed and wanted nothing more than to get out of here and away from these people. "When you called me Ange, it just took me back. That's the name I used to go by. That's the name my kidnapper said when he mocked me. He'd say it over and over while he…" She stopped. Those scars were for her eyes only. She didn't want anyone to experience that sort of thing, even vicariously. "I know it's ridiculous, but that's all it takes to make me fall apart."

Max smiled. "It's not that ridiculous. You don't know anything about us. Not really. Only what we say at the meeting. Any of us could be a crazed psycho killer for all you know."

Angelina's pulse soared.

"I don't think that's a useful thing to say, Max." Nate frowned. "And I'm sure it's not true. He's just joking, Angelina. None of us want to hurt you."

Max smiled at her. "But I'm only pointing out there's nothing wrong with being a little suspicious of people. Not everyone's trustworthy."

Nate stood and dusted off his pants then held a hand out to her.

A part of her wanted to ignore his outstretched hand. To get up on her own. But she couldn't do it alone. She did need help. But were these the people who could be trusted to help? They stood around her, protective, blocking out anyone who might try to hurt her.

She reached out and put her hand in Nate's.

15

Angelina's eyes popped open. Why was it dark? She always slept with a light on. She hated the dark. It reminded her of being trapped. She lay in bed listening. Something had awoken her. A noise?

"Ange," A soft voice whispered in the dark.

She blinked, sure she was still dreaming.

"Ange."

Had she really heard a voice? Impossible. She was on the second floor. Someone couldn't get in her apartment without her knowing it. Not a voice, maybe it was a tree branch brushing against her window. Except there were no trees nearby.

"Ange."

Definitely a voice. Not a tree branch. Someone was in her house. Her arm shot out to turn on the light. Instead, she knocked it off the nightstand. The sound of shattering glass echoed through the pitch-black room. She had to get out of here.

She fumbled around the night stand once more and found her phone. Jumping out of bed, she ran to the window. Peering out, all she saw was more darkness. The pole light was off. Had the electricity gone off? It happened sometimes out here in the country.

"Ange. Want to play?"

This couldn't be happening. It wasn't real. Had to be her imagination. She turned from the window and sank to the floor. He was here. In the apartment with her. She didn't know how it was possible, but he was back. And he would kill her this time if she didn't get out. But she couldn't make herself move. She was stuck. Trapped again. Without a way to protect herself. Why hadn't she bought a gun? She needed a gun. To kill Luther. She wouldn't let him hurt her again.

"Want to play, Ange?"

Tears streamed down her cheeks. She couldn't just sit here and wait for Luther to come and get her. She became aware of the phone she clutched in her hand. She hit the last number dialed.

"Nate Goodman."

"He's here. He's here. He's going to kill me," she cried.

"Angelina?"

"Yes, yes, it's me. Angelina. He's here. Going to kill me."

"Where are you?"

"M…my apartment."

"Be right there."

"Ange. Want to play?"

She clutched at the phone and threw it, hoping it would hit Luther. Wherever he was. She wouldn't let him touch her again. Ever. She'd die first.

Her gaze went to the window. If she could climb out, she could run to the main house for help. Keren and Peter could help her this time. It wouldn't be like last time. She wasn't alone. There were people who loved her.

She stood, but she was shaking so badly her legs could barely hold her up. Turning to the window, she tugged on it. Stuck. It wouldn't open.

"Ange, don't you want to play with me?"

The voice was closer. Forget about opening it, she moved from the window and then kicked it. As glass shattered, pain shot up her bare foot. After knocking away more glass, she stuck her head out, feeling the wind blowing her hair. She could breathe again.

She wouldn't wait for Luther to kill her. She put one leg through the window, then the other. Now she was balanced on the sill. She stared down at the ground. Such a long way.

"Ange, come play with me."

She wouldn't let Luther kidnap her again. She'd rather die. She took a deep breath —

"Angelina? What are you doing?" Keren stood by the door at the main house with a newspaper in her hand.

"Luther's in my apartment," she yelled. "He's going to kill me. I have to jump. I won't let him touch me again."

"Don't jump. You'll hurt yourself." Keren was running toward her.

"Keren. Don't come up here. Luther will kill you too."

Her cousin stopped running, her hands out in a pleading gesture. "Luther's dead, Angelina. Remember. He can't hurt you. He's dead. Please don't jump. It was a nightmare."

"It's not true. He's in here. He's going to kill me. I have to get out." She readied herself.

"Please don't jump."

"I have to." Her voice broke, tears clogging her throat and eyes. "I have to…"

Headlights turned into the drive. Nate. Nate would protect her — he'd keep her safe. The car stopped and Nate stepped out of the car.

"Nate. Luther's going to kill me."

His gaze moved upward, "Angelina, don't jump. I'll be right there."

"Ange. Are you ready to play? Here I come."

Luther would never touch her again.

~*~

"Don't move, Angelina. I'll come to you."

She shook her head. "No. Won't let him hurt me again."

Nate looked at Keren. "Can you get in her apartment?"

"Yes."

"Go." Even as he said the word everything telescoped to focus totally on her.

Keren ran toward the stairs of the apartment.

Angelina shifted, her bare feet dangling, blood dripping from one foot. She took a deep breath, looking into some hell only she could see.

"Nooooo…" Nate ran as she dropped through the air and his arms went out as she hurtled toward him.

~*~

Angelina opened her eyes. She was curled up on her bed in her old room at the main house. Why was she here? So tired…too tired to think. Her eyes drooped, but she forced them open. Something….something…she struggled to remember. "Keren?"

A moment later the door opened with Dr. Markley coming into her room.

What was going on?

The doctor looked concerned. "How are you, Angelina?"

She had no idea how to answer. "What happened? Why are you here?"

"You don't remember?"

"Remember what?" Even as she said the words, the memory came back. Luther. Nate. The window. Along with the memories came the panic. "Luther. Luther was in my apartment. He was going to kill me."

"Luther wasn't in your house." The doctor's voice was calm, reassuring. "But you thought he was. No one was in the apartment with you. You were safe the whole time. It must have been a dream. A nightmare."

That was ridiculous. It had been real. She'd heard his voice—his horrible whisper. "It wasn't a dream. I heard him. I was awake when I got out of the bed. He was there. He was going to kill me." Why didn't the doctor believe her?

"Our minds can play tricks on us sometimes, Angelina. Haven't you ever had a dream where you thought you woke up only to realize you were still dreaming?"

She had. Real or not real? She wasn't sure. The whole thing did have a bizarre dream-like quality to it. Could it really have been a nightmare? "No. I...I think it was real."

"But you aren't sure?"

"I...I...it seemed real then. Now I'm not...not so sure."

"The sleeping pill you use has a history of causing sleepwalking incidents just like this."

"You really think it was a dream and that I was walking in my sleep?"

"I do." The doctor nodded. "I'll prescribe a different sleeping pill so you won't have any more episodes like last night. That should do the trick. There shouldn't be any more sleepwalking events. I'm so sorry this happened, but it wasn't real."

"I guess. But...but...I'm not sure that's what happened. But I wasn't sleeping, I was awake. I heard him call my name right before I jumped. I saw Nate and Keren. That part wasn't a dream." She knew what she heard. Luther was calling her name. Asking if she wanted to play games with him. That had been real, not a dream. "Nate was there, right?"

"Thankfully, he was. If he hadn't caught you, you could have been really hurt."

"I called him. On the phone. That means I wasn't dreaming. I didn't just call him in my dream. It was real."

"That part was real, but Luther wasn't in your apartment. He's dead, so it's impossible." Dr. Markley watched her carefully.

"But I jumped out of the window. Nate caught me, right?"

The doctor nodded.

"So that part wasn't a dream. So what makes you think Luther being in my house was a dream?"

"Because Luther Marks is dead," Nate said as he walked in the room. "Remember? Leslie shot him. He's dead, Angelina. He can't hurt you ever again."

She stared at him and then pointed. "Did I do that?"

"No big deal." He held up the arm in the sling. "A sprained shoulder. The doctor just wanted me to keep my arm immobilized to make sure it doesn't get any worse."

"First you get shot in the shoulder because of me, and now I jumped on top of you. You saved me. Again. I'm sorry."

"Better me than the concrete drive." He grinned.

"I can't believe I did that. I'm so sorry, Nate." She took a deep breath. "But I'm telling you. Luther Marks was in my apartment with me. I heard his voice. His whisper. And the same words. 'Want to play a game?' He kept saying it over and over. You believe me, right?"

His gaze met hers.

She needed him to believe her. That she wasn't nuts. She wouldn't just jump out of a window for no reason.

His smile reassured her. He looked at Dr. Markley. "I need to talk with Angelina. Alone. If you don't mind."

Dr. Markley shook her head. "I don't think that's a good idea. She doesn't have a good grasp of reality right now. Anything—"

"She has a perfectly fine grasp of reality, don't you?"

Tears filled her eyes. Nate believed her. Even if no one else did. "Luther's dead. He wasn't in my house. It was a nightmare."

Dr. Markley nodded. "I'll be right outside if you need me."

After the door closed, Nate walked over and sat on the bed. "You trust me, right?"

"Of course. That's why I called you." She grinned. "Well, that and the fact your number was the last number dialed. But I was so scared. I didn't know what to do so I called you."

"And I'm so glad you did." He touched her arm.

That was all it took. Her own arms went around his neck. "I'm telling you the truth. That man was in my apartment. I heard him asking if I wanted to play his sick little games again."

He pulled her close. "Take a few breaths, Angelina. Deep ones."

She did. As she calmed down, she moved her head to his shoulder. He caressed her hair. It felt so good to have him hold her. So safe. Eventually, she moved away. "Do you believe me, Nate?"

"I want to tell you about my last case as a Chicago policeman. Can I do that?"

She nodded.

When he was finished, he looked at her. "For months afterward, I would hear that little girl crying for help. Not thinking about it. Not imagining it. But actually hearing it."

"Just the way I heard Luther?"

He nodded. "So I'm not telling you that you were imagining it or dreaming it. I understand completely. You heard what you heard. But Dr. Markley's right when she says our mind can play tricks on us. It wasn't Luther. It was your mind. And it doesn't mean you're crazy; it means you have PTSD. Do you believe me?"

She met his gaze. "I believe you."

"Good. Now I want you to listen and follow the doctor's orders. She knows what she's doing. After all, she helped me."

"She helped you?"

"She did. I'll tell you all about it someday. But doctors can only do so much. God has to be a part of your recovery as well. That's why I'm so glad you're coming to the support group at the church."

She nodded. This wasn't the time to tell him that she had no plans to go to another meeting after that anxiety attack. She didn't need any more humiliation. *The anxiety attack?* Maybe that was why she'd had the nightmare. "OK, tell Dr. Markley to come back in."

He leaned down and kissed her cheek. "You're getting better, Angelina. I did and so can you. With God, all things are possible." He left.

Dr. Markley walked back in.

Angelina smiled at her. "OK, I've calmed down. Of course, I know Luther Marks is dead and that he can't hurt me anymore. And as real as it seemed, it must have been a nightmare. Just as you said."

"That's good to hear."

"How did you get here?"

"Keren called me. Said you were hysterical. I gave you a shot to calm you down. She tells me you've been going to support meetings. How's that going?"

"Apparently not well if I'm having these nightmares. And I had an anxiety attack last night after the meeting. That might be what triggered the nightmare."

"Quite possibly. Well, keep going. You've just got to give it time."

He restoreth my soul.

She couldn't do this alone. But with God, all things were possible. "You're right. I've given Luther Marks enough of my time. I'm not giving him any more of it." She sat up, feeling stronger than she ever had. Luther wouldn't win.

"That's the right attitude. How about we walk back over to your apartment together. That way you can see it's safe."

It would be safer to be here with Keren and Peter. Even if it was a nightmare, she could have another, and try to jump out the window again. Of course, this room had windows, too.

Keren stood in the doorway. "I think she should just move in here. After all, it is your house, Angelina. And you'll be safer here. And we can be together."

"She's safe there." Dr. Markley's voice was firm. "It's just as safe in her apartment as it is in this house. But it's up to you, Angelina. Do you want to move forward or go backward?"

If she stayed here, that would be a step backward. Got to keep moving forward. It was the only way to get un-trapped. "I don't think that's a good idea, Keren. The doctor's right. I've got to learn to live on my own again."

"I don't know about that. Even Peter agrees that you should be staying here. In your own house. Not in that ridiculously tiny apartment."

Dr. Markley watched Angelina. She shrugged. "It's up to you. But it's important to keep moving forward."

She needed to fix the broken watch—her life. Get it ticking again. Taking a deep breath, Angelina got out of bed. "Then let's go check my apartment."

16

Angelina walked around her apartment. She'd triple-checked all the windows. All two of them. One in the living room and the one she'd jumped out of in the bedroom—fixed and safe.

After Nate and Dr. Markley left, it had been a busy day. Not only had the repairman fixed the window, but the security company had been out and installed a security system in her apartment. They assured her that they'd be out in a heartbeat if the windows or the doors were tampered with. Nobody could get in. Unless she invited them or they had the code. And she'd only given Keren and Peter the code.

She'd been too busy to think about Nate's kiss, but now it was replaying in her mind. That soft touch on her cheek had...awakened something inside her. It had been a friendly gesture. A quick peck to show he cared. He wasn't like any of her previous boyfriends. He wasn't rich or famous, but he was...real. Nate was such a good and godly man. Of course, such a man wouldn't be interested in her. Not after most of her exploits had been televised. But still, the thought of her and Nate together made her smile. "Stop it, Angelina. No sense thinking about something that will never happen." Just having Nate as a friend was more than she deserved.

Time to go to bed.

After checking the doors and windows a fourth

time, she slipped into bed. She fought the urge to keep the light on. She touched the lamp and the room darkened. In the next instant, both nightlights in the room came to life giving off a soft glow. Enough to allow her to see there was no one in the room with her.

Another baby step forward. Lamp off—nightlights on.

The electrician also come out that day, changed all the fuses, and assured her they wouldn't go off again. As long as she wasn't in complete dark, she'd be OK. She took several deep breaths and closed her eyes.

"Ange," the whisper seemed all around her.

"It's not real. You're not real. You're dead and you can't hurt me."

"Ange, do you want to play?" the whispered response was evil.

Breathe in—breathe out. Slowly deeply. Not real. Keeping her eyes closed, she refused to give into the terror. And eventually she fell asleep.

When Angelina opened her eyes, light streamed in the window she'd jumped out of yesterday. She stared at it. If Nate hadn't been there, she'd have been seriously hurt. But Nate had been there. Again.

She smiled at the thought of him but then the reality of the day broke through. Angelina wanted to stay in bed. The anxiety attack at the meeting, and then the nightmare, had destroyed her moving forward with her life. And she'd heard Luther's voice again last night.

The voice seemed so real. She wondered if she should just put the covers over her head and accept her fate. Move back in the house with Keren and Peter and let them take care of her. The rich, crazy woman that everyone in town would pity.

Maybe Keren was right. She kept saying Angelina was moving too fast. But she'd heard Luther calling out to her last night and hadn't jumped out the window. Thanks to Nate, she'd refused to give into the terror. Maybe there was still hope for her.

It was a victory that she'd not again succumbed to the voice in the dark. Hopefully only the first.

Tears filled her eyes as she reached for the support group index cards on her night stand.

With God, all things are possible.

She read it again and again. Did she believe that? Or was she giving up because it was hard?

The past few weeks had been filled with progress. Lots of baby steps as Nate would say. Going to the group. Volunteering at school. Coffee and doughnuts with Nate. Not jumping out the window last night.

All progress. Victory.

Nate being one of the leaders of the support group was a shock. No wonder he'd been so kind, so compassionate toward her, He'd had his own demons to face. And he'd succeeded.

And what about Rosie, and Max, and Fred? If they could do it, why couldn't she? After all they were in the process of succeeding.

Thinking of Fred, she remembered she needed to call the plant manager. She should have done it yesterday but with all that happened, it had slipped her mind. At least she could do that much for someone. She grabbed her phone from the nightstand.

After the call, she stared at the index card.

With God all things are possible.

Just because she wouldn't be going back to the group didn't mean she couldn't get healthy.

And with God that could happen—no it would

happen.

She'd made progress and she meant to continue.

Seeing the kids would be good. They made her smile. She was ready to read to them that morning so she could forget all about the past few days. She'd discovered how much she enjoyed being with children. It was amazing—and fun to watch them be themselves. Had she ever been that carefree? Probably. But certainly not lately. But she wasn't giving up just because she'd had a bad day.

With God, all things are possible.

She got out of bed. After a shower and breakfast, she found enough energy to go to school. After reading, she stopped at Charles's desk. "Hey Charles, how are you today?"

He looked up, his eyes wide.

What had happened to make this little boy so frightened of the world?

"I'm OK," he whispered.

She knelt down beside him. "Sorry, I didn't choose you today, but I can't pick you every time. That wouldn't be fair to the other kids."

"I know." He smiled, his voice so soft she could barely hear him.

Her heart hurt for him. Life shouldn't be so scary for children—or for adults either. But then again, the world was a scary place. Maybe she could make it a little less scary for him. "Would you like to help me carry my books to my car?"

He nodded.

"Let me ask Miss Dawkins."

A moment later, she handed him two of the lightest books. Everything about the little boy seemed fragile, much like the way she felt. They left the classroom.

"So, Charlie...is it OK if I call you Charlie? You look more like a Charlie than a Charles."

His gaze moved up to her. "I guess. But if you want you can call me Carlos."

"Why would I call you that?"

"It's my other name."

"You mean your middle name?"

"I don't know. Mama used to call me Carlos, but now she calls me Charlie, too."

"So, Charlie–Carlos, what do you like to do for fun?"

"I don't know."

Her mind searched for a topic that he'd respond to. "Do you like football or are you more of a soccer guy?"

"I don't know."

"Well which one do you play with more? A soccer ball or a football?"

"I don't have a ball."

"Oh, that's too bad."

"Mama says toys are a waste of money. But I do have some books."

She held open the door, and he walked outside. "Well, this won't work, Charlie–Carlos. You have to hold the door open, or we'll both get locked out."

He giggled. "That would be funny."

She laughed along with him. "That would NOT be funny. You hold the door, and I'll be back in a minute." She ran down the steps, put the books in the car, and then went back to the door. She reached to get his books. He turned his head away—almost cowering. Angelina's stomach knotted. "Oops, sorry. Didn't mean to scare you, Charlie–Carlos. I just wanted the books."

He handed them to her without a word.

"I'll be right back. Don't even think about shutting that door, Charlie–Carlos."

He smiled, but the light was gone from his eyes.

Once again, she trotted out to her car, and then returned to the door.

Charles-Carlos held the door open with a solemn expression.

"Thanks so much, Charlie–Carlos. Couldn't have done it without you."

He motioned for her to come closer so she knelt down beside him.

"Better not call me that. I forgot that Mama told me not to tell anyone about that name. It's a secret. Nobody's 'sposed to know I'm Carlos."

She didn't like the sound of that. Kids weren't supposed to keep those kinds of secrets. "Oh...OK, then I'll just call you Charlie." After walking him back to his classroom, Angelina went straight to the principal's office.

The woman looked up from her paper work. "Oh, Miss Matthews. How're things going?"

"Oh, really good. The kids are great. I really enjoy reading to them and talking with them."

"That's good to hear. Is there something you needed?"

"Well...I...ah...was wondering. Would it be appropriate for me to buy one of the students a few books, and maybe a soccer ball?"

The principal looked at Angelina over her glasses. "Mmm...I'm not sure that's the best idea, Ms. Matthews. It could cause a problem. The other children might get jealous. Who's the child?"

"Charles Wright."

"He's a strange little one, isn't he?"

"Sort of. He told me today that he didn't have a soccer ball or a football. His mom thinks toys are a waste of money. So I'm guessing that means they can't afford it. Every kid should have a ball, don't you think?"

"I see. No wonder you wanted to buy him a few things." She shook her head. "I know it seems like a harmless thing to do, but I'm glad you checked with me. I'm afraid it might cause more problems than it would solve."

How could buying a child a gift cause a problem? Of course, she wasn't an expert. "I'm worried that he might be getting abused. At home. Or maybe being bullied here at school."

"Really." The principal took off her glasses and stared. "Why would you think that? I haven't had any reports about it. The teachers are mandated to report any signs of abuse. "

"I'm sure it's nothing, but when I reached for the books he was holding for me, he sort of cowered away from me. As if he thought I would hit him or something."

"Some kids are like that, but we can't be too careful about such things. I'll tell the teacher to be on the lookout for bruises or anything unusual. And to watch for how the other students treat him." She tapped her fingers on the desk. "But I'm sure he's fine. Otherwise the teacher would have told me so."

"Of course. By the way, do you know Officer Goodman?"

Her eyes narrowed. "There's no reason to get him involved in the matter. In fact, there's no need for him to get involved at this point. As I said, we'll keep an eye on Charles."

She shook her head. "Oh, no. That's not why I was asking. He's a...he's a friend. I just wondered if he was here today. I saw him last week when I was here and wanted to say hi if he was around today."

"Oh, I see." Her tone returned to friendly. "Nate is so wonderful with the kids. They all love him."

"Is he here today?"

She held up a finger as she walked toward her door. "Hold on. Let me check." A moment later she was back. "Not here. He won't be back until Thursday. I guess one week he does a Tuesday and the next a Thursday."

"Thanks." Angelina was surprised at her disappointment.

"Thank you for being so concerned about little Charles. And I'll tell the teacher to keep an eye open for any problems. We want all of our students to feel safe. Here and at their home."

Angelina walked out to her car. She'd been looking forward to seeing Nate again. Or maybe she just wanted an excuse for a doughnut. A few minutes later, she pulled into the bakery parking lot. She perused the array of tasty treats.

"Imagine finding you at the doughnut shop." A man came from behind her.

She grinned. "It's your fault. I had no idea the doughnuts here were so good. I decided to treat myself to one."

"Me, too. Or maybe three. It's important to fuel this body, you know?" Nate patted his stomach.

"Well if I keep stopping here, I might have to start working out. Too much fuel isn't a good thing."

"You don't need to do that. Your body is just fine." His face turned pink. "I...never mind. Anything I say now won't sound any better." He winked.

She touched his sling. "How's your shoulder?"

"I'll live."

"That bad?"

"Not at all, but I was thinking I could use it to wrangle up a little pity from you."

The waitress walked over. "That will be two fifty."

Angelina handed her a ten. "I'll pay for what he wants, too. It's the least I can do."

When they were settled at the table, Nate took a huge bite from his glazed doughnut. "All the doughnuts are good, but I love the glazed ones."

"I can see that."

"I'm glad to see you out and about."

"Because of yesterday?"

He nodded. "I was afraid you'd get discouraged. Give up."

"That's exactly what I planned to do, but I started reading my Bible verses from the group. They helped."

"Nothing like God's Word to keep us on the right track."

"It's all about those baby steps you and Dr. Markley keep talking about. But yesterday wasn't about baby steps forward. I went backward—lots of giant steps backward."

"That's the way it happened with me, too. I'll think I'm finally over it, and then something would trigger a memory, and I'd be stuck in the darkness again. The important thing is to keep your eyes on Jesus. And to not let yourself get trapped in the bad moments."

She wished she had that kind of faith. "I'll try

but…it's so hard. I can't believe I actually jumped out of the window for something that wasn't even really happening."

His gaze turned serious. "It was happening. In your mind. You have to give yourself the time you need to heal. And Dr. Markley is really good at her job. If she says it was the meds, then it probably was the meds. So there's nothing for you to be concerned about."

"But it felt so real. I heard the voice again last night but kept telling myself it wasn't real. I can't believe it, but eventually, I fell asleep." She sighed. "Let's talk about something else. I was really shocked when you walked into the meeting the other night. I had no idea you were the other group leader."

"Yeah, I was a little shocked to see you as well. Cooper had told me there were two new members, but I had no idea one of them was you. I guess I should have thought about it when you told me you were going to a support group. The group works. And this group has some really great members." After taking a drink of coffee, he looked at her. "Speaking of members, I wonder what will happen if Fred follows through on putting the application in to Diamond."

"Hopefully, good things." She smiled. "I forgot to call yesterday, but I called first thing this morning."

"That's really nice of you."

"It wasn't that big of a deal. Cooper said we create our own life by our actions. So I'm trying to sow some good seeds. And please don't tell Fred that I had anything to do with it. I'd rather he not know."

"Wouldn't think of it, but that doesn't sound much like the Angelina I used to hear about."

She grinned as she took a bite of her cream-filled

doughnut. "Good. I don't like that person very much anymore. So how did you end up as one of the group leaders?"

"I told you what happened with the little girl. What I didn't tell you is that I fell apart after that."

She nodded. "I can imagine."

"I quit my job and decided to start drinking instead. I was quite the mess and ended up in a homeless shelter. But I found God there. Eventually I found my way back home to Mt. Pleasant. And the rest is history." He popped the last of the doughnut in his mouth as he reach for his coffee cup. "But I couldn't have done any of it without God."

"Wow. That's pretty impressive."

"I'm not the one to be impressed with. It's all God. With God, all things really are possible. So, what's going on with you today?"

That was the exact verse that had gotten her out of bed. "Just finished up at school and I had a discussion with the principal. I'm not so sure she was happy with me."

"Why not?"

"I expressed some concerns about one of the little boys in the class I work in."

"What kind of concerns?" His tone turned serious.

"Well, first, he barely speaks above a whisper when he talks, which isn't much. Today I reached for the books he was holding for me, and he cowered as though he thought I would hit him. And then, the really odd thing is, he told me he used to have another name but it was a secret."

"Another name?" He arched a brow. "That is odd. I'm surprised Margaret wasn't more concerned."

"I didn't actually tell her that part. About the

name. I just told her he might be getting bullied at school or at home."

Angelina discussed her misgivings.

"I think I'll make sure I go to that classroom on Thursday and make sure little Charlie and I have a little alone time," Nate said with a small frown.

"Thanks. That will make me feel better. Can you call and let me know what you think?"

"Sure, but I warn you that I might call you for dinner on Friday night. Unless you have other plans."

17

After reading to the kids in Miss Dawkins' room, Nate headed to the principal's office. He stuck his head in. "Am I interrupting you?"

"Yes, you are. You're stopping me from the endless mountain of paperwork." She stood. "So you are a very welcome interruption."

"I know what you mean. It seems as if that's all my job is these days."

"What can I do for you, Nate?"

"I was in Miss Dawkins room and—"

"Let me guess. You're concerned about Charles Wright. Right?" The look on her face told him he was busted.

He nodded. "OK, let's not play games. Angelina Matthews came to me with some concerns. But I've got to tell you after talking with little Charlie, I share them."

She sat back down. "Fine, tell me about it."

"He tells me he used to have another name. He remembers being called Carlos but he can't remember his last name. And his mother told him that it was a secret name. That he shouldn't tell anybody about it. That's a little odd, don't you think?"

"Sometimes kids go by cute little nicknames until they start school. Or some of their family calls them one name while others call them something different. It's not really out of the ordinary."

"I suppose. But I'd like to take a look at his records anyway. If you don't mind."

She tapped her index fingers together forming a moving steeple. "I'm not sure if I should do that. I mean the records are private."

"Instead of me looking then why don't you have a look? See if anything stands out to you."

"I guess I could do that." She hit some keys on the computer. "Mmm. That's interesting."

"What's that?"

"No birth certificate. No previous school records. The only documentation the mother gave us was her current electric bill. To prove she lived in the district."

"Isn't that odd?"

"A bit odd, but sometimes that happens. Parents lose or don't have one initially, and have to order it from wherever the child was born. We take the child into the system, and when the parent receives the BC, they bring it to us. Hold on a minute. Maybe my assistant forgot to scan them. Let me check." She walked out of the office but was back within a few minutes, holding a paper file. "According to Darlene, when the mother registered Charles, she'd explained that the office that had her child's BC had a fire and the records were destroyed. And he was a kindergartener at the time so he hadn't been enrolled in any other school before. A few states still don't have mandatory kindergarten. The mother promised she'd get a copy of his medical records sent to us."

"But she never did, right?"

"Never did."

"I thought you had to have proof of immunizations."

Margaret nodded and looked through the papers

in the file. "They are here, but they were done in town by a local doctor. And only after we asked for them." She looked up at him. "It's not as if she did anything wrong. She followed the law but...what do you think it means?"

"I'm not sure yet. But I'll look into it and let you know. In the meantime, let's keep this between ourselves."

An hour later Nate stared at the computer screen in his office. No info on Charles or his mother, Bonnie Wright. There didn't appear to be any social media presence for either of them, a rarity these days.

When he'd asked Charles about the name Carlos, he'd told Nate that he couldn't remember any other part of the name. Nate went to the missing child network. The FBI kept a database of every missing child in the country. He typed in the name CARLOS.

18

As Angelina pulled in to her drive, Keren peeked out and waved from the back deck. After parking, Angelina joined her on the deck. "Hey. You look like you're enjoying yourself."

"I admit that I am." Keren took a sip of lemonade. "Hey, I guess you're feeling better, huh? I was surprised to find you gone. I thought you'd just want to hang around here."

"It was my day to read with the kids."

"Ahhh. I didn't expect you to go. Not after everything that happened yesterday."

"Yeah, yesterday was a bad day. But you know what? It was only one day."

"I guess. I just wanted to thank you for the cleaning lady. She's awesome. Gives me a little time to sit out here and enjoy the day." She pointed at the book sitting on the little wooden table beside her glass of lemonade.

"No problem. I should have thought of it sooner."

"I can send her over to your apartment next time if you'd like?"

"Not necessary. I sort of like learning how to clean. The first time I used the vacuum cleaner I wasn't sure who was going to win. Me or it." She laughed. "But I'm getting the hang of it."

"There's no reason you should be getting better at it. You're rich. Take advantage of it. I know I would. I hate cleaning."

"It's time for me to grow up a little. I might even buy a cook book and learn how to cook something besides scrambled eggs." For a moment, she was back in that house with Luther as she'd begged him to let her cook for him. She brushed the memory away. Thinking of Rosie, she said, "Maybe I'll start with cookies."

"I really wish you'd change your mind and move back in here. In your own house. There's no reason—"

"It's part of the whole growing up thing."

"If you say so." Keren rolled her eyes.

"Speaking of growing up, we need to have a little talk."

"About what?"

"I really appreciate all you've done for me. Taking care of me, moving down here so I wasn't completely alone. All of it."

"Uh-oh. That sounds ominous."

"Not at all. I just want you to know how much I appreciate you. But…" She grinned at her cousin. "But I am an adult. And I do need to…never mind. I just wanted to remind you I'm an adult, and you don't really need to worry about me every minute of the day. It's really not your job."

Keren stared at her for a moment. "OK, if you say so, but that's easier said than done. Want to eat dinner with us tonight? You seem as if you're always busy anymore. No time for your family."

"What's on the menu?"

"Well, I haven't started dinner yet so what would you like?"

"In that case, how about we go out to eat?" It had been a long time since she'd gone out for dinner. The doughnut shop with Nate didn't technically count, since it wasn't dinner.

Keren wrinkled her nose, and then sighed. "Probably not."

"Why?"

"Money's a little tight. I might as well tell you Peter lost his job. The company cut ten percent of their work force. And, of course, since he hadn't worked there all that long…" She sighed. "So, no restaurants for the time being. And I might have to go look for a job myself if he doesn't find one soon."

"Oh, I didn't know. I'm so sorry. Dinner will be my treat. It's the least I can do after scaring the wits out of both of you yesterday. If that's OK?"

"Sure. If you want. Now that he's laid off, Peter can get to some of the things around the house that need to be done, anyway. He might as well put his time to good use. There's a ton of things that need some work. Nothing big, just small things."

"Oh, I suppose there is." She looked around the backyard, feeling slightly guilty. She really hadn't done a whole lot to take care of this place lately.

"Nothing major, Angelina. But it's still a good idea to keep up with them. Of course, we might need to borrow a little money from you for supplies, but he's glad to do the work for free."

"I wouldn't hear of it. And you're right, we've always had a few staff around here when I was growing up, so maybe that's what we need to do again. Tell Peter, he's officially hired. If he wants the job."

"You are too sweet. But it's not necessary. You've already done so much for us. Letting us live in this beautiful house. We'll be OK, financially. I'm sure he'll find a job soon, and his DJ work helps. In fact, he has a gig tomorrow night. In Akron. Want to go with us?"

"No, thanks and it is necessary. I own the house. It's my duty to keep it in good shape. Tell him we can talk about his salary at dinner. See you later—about six." She walked off the deck and toward her apartment.

Her cell phone started ringing as she went up the stairs to her apartment. She rummaged through her phone and quickly pressed the button. "Hi, Nate."

"How'd you know it was me?"

"I programmed your number in my phone."

"Oh, yeah. Anyway, I talked with little Charlie Wright, and I think you might be right. You told me he'd carried a few books for you."

"Yeah?"

"Think I can see those books."

"Why?"

"I'd like to compare his prints with some missing children."

She couldn't breathe. "You think he was kidnapped?"

"It's only one possibility, but I did find some missing children named Carlos in his age group. I can stop by and get the books."

"No need. I'll bring them to you right now."

"You don't—"

"Oh, yes I do." Twenty minutes later, she walked into the Mt. Pleasant police station.

Nate was sitting in an office, but the moment he saw her, he stood and motioned for her to come in. "Thanks for coming so quickly."

"Well, of course. It's important." She looked around the office. "I only see this one office, and it says Chief of Police. Is it your office?"

"Yeah, they promoted me when Leslie left to join the FBI. You remember Leslie, right?"

She nodded. "I had no idea you're the Chief of Police. Now I'm really impressed. I can't believe you didn't tell me you were promoted."

"Don't be. I probably only got it because of you anyway."

"Because of me?"

"You and timing. Leslie left a few weeks after the incident with Luther Marks."

"You mean when you saved me," she corrected.

"Only Jesus saves. I found you. Anyway, with all the headlines and news about it, they must have decided it would be best to promote me instead of hunting for a new chief."

"Well, at least something good came from..." She hated even saying his name. Baby steps. She took a deep breath. "Luther Marks. Plus, I'm sure you're the right man for the job. You probably would have gotten the promotion anyway."

"I don't know about that but so far so good. Speaking of which, let's take a look at those books. Are they library books? If they are, they'll have a ton of fingerprints on them."

"No. I actually just bought them. They probably only have mine and Charlie's prints on them."

"Great."

"What will you do? Send them to some forensic place or something to be examined?"

"Nah. That would take too much time. A little old-fashioned police work. This isn't for a trial. I just want to compare with some of the missing kids' prints from the national database. If we find anything that looks close to the same, we'll go from there."

She handed him the two books. "Can I watch?"

"Sure." He walked over to a cupboard and pulled out a bottle. "This should do the trick. This is fingerprint powder. It's bi-chromatic which means it will show up light on dark surfaces and dark on lighter-colored surfaces."

"Interesting."

He shook the jar of powder, then opened it and twirled the brush in the lid. "It's not good to use too much of the powder. It'll actually mess up the print. So I always go with the less is more philosophy." He gently swirled the brush across the book. He repeated the process one more time and then held the book up with a smile. The book cover had several prints on it. He walked back to the cupboard. "This is fingerprint tape. But first we need to see which is yours and which is Charlie's."

She stared at the book cover and pointed at one. "I think that's his. It's smaller than the other ones. Plus that's probably where he held the book."

He nodded. "I agree. You've got a good eye. Maybe you should take up police work."

She laughed. "I don't think so."

Nate opened his drawer and pulled out a small camera. He snapped several pictures of the print. "Just in case I mess up, we can use the photo if we have to." Using a piece of the fingerprint tape, he pressed it against the print. He took a ruler from his pencil holder and ran it across the tape. After that he lifted the tape as if it were a bandage, one quick motion. Then he pressed the tape against a small white card. "This is a fingerprint backing card." He examined it and then held it up so she could see it. "Not bad if I say so myself."

"Wow. That's pretty cool. Now what?"

"Now I compare it to prints of the missing Carloses. They're already on my computer." He walked over and sat down and then stood again. "You sit. I can look over your shoulder."

"Don't be silly. I'm just watching. You're the one who knows what they're doing. Sit."

He'd narrowed it down by age group as well as race. Still, there were more than twenty candidates who had the first or middle name of Carlos or Charles. Her heart broke as Nate compared fingerprint after fingerprint. How could there be that many missing children with the name Carlos?

Finally, he looked up. "This one looks close. What do you think?"

She leaned down, staring between the screen and the fingerprint on the card. "I don't know. It looks like a lot of squiggles to me."

"That's what they are but look closely." He ran his finger over the screen. "See that line. Probably a small scar." He held up the card. "This one has the same scar in the same place."

Her heart pounded. Little Charlie really was a kidnap victim. Unbelievable. "What's his real name?"

"Carlos Perez." He pressed a button.

"He's really a kidnapped child?"

"No, not kidnapped. Both he and his mother are listed as missing persons." Nate clicked on a button.

The fingerprint was replaced with a picture of a sweet-looking, chubby toddler being held by a young woman. Angelina squinted at the name. Bonita Perez. "Why are they listed as missing?"

"I'm not sure. All this gives is a number to call if they're found."

"Are you going to call?"

"Of course."

Why were they listed as missing? It didn't make sense. "But shouldn't we find out why they're missing first and who's looking for them?"

"I'm sure I'll find out more when I call."

"Maybe she doesn't want to be found. She could have been in an abusive situation or something like that. Can't you go find out more on your own? Before you call."

"I don't really see a reason to do that. Someone must be very worried about them. This will put their mind at ease."

"I need to go, Nate. See you later." She headed for the door.

"Everything OK?"

Her feet stopped. "What do you mean?"

"One minute you're all involved, and now you seem as though you can't wait to leave." Even though his tone was calm, his gaze demanded an answer.

Should she tell him? "Well...I...uh...I'm not sure."

"Not sure about what?"

She shrugged. "I don't know. It's just a feeling. She's an adult. Doesn't she have a right to decide who she's in contact with?"

"But think about it, Angelina. If I'd ignored Keren when she came in and filed a missing person's report on you, who knows what would have happened?"

"Well that's true, but what if she doesn't want to be found?"

~*~

Nate didn't have a chance to ask another question. Angelina hurried out of the station.

What if Carlos' mother didn't want to be found?

Nate didn't like the sound of that. Certainly Angelina wouldn't do something she might regret later. Maybe it just reminded her too much of her own kidnapping and she needed a breath of fresh air. He hoped it wasn't another setback. She was improving every day, not just from the ordeal, but in her personal life.

She seemed to be intent on becoming a different person. And he liked that person. A lot. More than he should. But he also knew this wasn't the time in Angelina's life for her to get involved romantically with someone—not even him.

Her focus needed to be on her—on getting healthy.

He did enjoy being around her, though. *Focus, Goodman, on the task at hand.* He picked up the phone to call the number listed on the missing person's report but stopped.

What if she doesn't want to be found?

It was his job to make the call. Even as he pressed the numbers, a part of him wondered if he was doing the right thing.

19

Angelina followed the yellow school bus, feeling a bit like a stalker. But it was for a good cause. She needed to meet Charlie's mom, figure out why someone thought they were missing. She couldn't really explain why, but it seemed important.

By now it was probably out of her hands. Surely, Nate had already called the number. Or even the FBI. Maybe not. Did all missing person's reports go through the FBI? She had no idea.

Still, she kept following the bus. It left the town and headed out onto the rural roads dropping off children every few houses. Most of the kids would turn back around and give a big wave to their friends.

Eventually, Charlie-Carlos stepped off the bus. He didn't turn and wave at friends like all the other kids. Instead, he ran across the road and up toward an old white farmhouse that had seen better days. It was in need of paint, but the yard was trimmed and well-tended.

The door opened. A woman stepped out and waved at the bus driver.

As the bus drove off, Angelina wondered what to do. Should she follow the bus? Or take a chance? She turned into the drive.

Charlie ran to the woman who leaned down and hugged him. He hugged her back.

They both focused on Angelina as she stepped out of the car. Now that she was here, she wasn't sure what to say or do. "Hi."

"Go in the house, Charlie." The woman's face twitched.

"Miss Angelina." He turned to his mother. "This is the nice lady from school who reads to me. Remember I—"

"Go in the house, Charlie."

"But Mama—"

"Now, Charlie."

He did as he was told.

She looked at Angelina. "Can I help you?" Her tone wasn't friendly, but it wasn't rude either. Just cautious.

"Ah, yeah, I guess you can. I work at the school. Well, actually I don't work, I volunteer. Anyway, I was behind the bus and saw Charlie get off. Just thought I'd stop in and meet you. Charlie's one of my favorites. He's such a sweet boy."

"He is a good boy." The woman turned and motioned for Charlie to come back out. He was peeking out the door. "Charlie, do you know her?"

He nodded. "She reads books to us. And she let me help her carry the books out. She's nice."

When she turned back toward Angelina some of the tension had seeped out. "I wish I had time to help out at Charlie's school, but paying the bills comes first."

"Of course." She held out her hand. "I'm Angelina Matthews."

"Bonnie Wright, Charlie's mom." Bonnie Wright? That wasn't the name on the report. It was Bonita Perez, but it was close enough. Wright could be her maiden name.

The two women stared at each other. So now what should she say? *Oh, by the way, why are you calling yourself and your son by different names?* Instead, she said, "I'm sorry I know I shouldn't have just popped in like this. I don't even know what I was thinking."

"It was nice of you."

Angelina pointed at her car. "I guess I'd better go."

"Would you like to come in for a minute?"

Perfect. The woman was probably only asking out of politeness, but she might be able to find out more information if they had a conversation. "I'd love that. How long have you lived here? It's a darling house."

"Since last year. We moved around some before that, but once it was time for Charlie to start school, I decided we needed to find a place to stay put."

"You made a good choice." That didn't sound like a bad mother. "Mt. Pleasant is a nice place to raise children. Do you have any other children?"

Bonnie Wright shook her head. "No, just me and Charlie."

"Well, you seem to be doing a great job with him. He's a good boy."

Bonnie held the door open as Angelina walked in. She had to find a way to…to what? She was way out of her league here. She wasn't even sure what she wanted to accomplish. She blurted out, "Does his father live around here, too?"

Bonnie's eyes turned hard, and then she shook her head. "Charlie's father died. A car accident when he was not quite a year old." She patted Charlie's head. "But he loved Charlie so much, didn't he?"

Charlie nodded. "I gotta picture of him. Want to see it?"

"Sure."

Charlie ran out of the room.

Was Bonnie telling the truth or was that just a story she'd told Charlie? Or was he the person who'd reported them missing? Was Charlie's father out there searching for him? "I'm so sorry for your loss."

"It's been tough. That's really the reason we traveled around so much. I needed some time and space to mourn. Sometimes, it's hard to do that around family. They can expect so…so much from you." There was a ring of truth in her voice.

Angelina believed her. "That's true, but sometimes it's good to have family around too." She couldn't have survived her ordeal without Keren and Peter.

"I guess it depends on the family."

"That's for sure." Angelina looked around the room. Clean and tidy. "Where do you work?"

"I work at two different jobs. I work at The Parlor for the day shift and then I clean Simpson's Law offices in the evening. After we eat supper, we go back in town. Charlie does his homework while I clean."

Shame flooded Angelina. She'd never worked a day in her life, and here this woman was working two jobs so she could provide a home for her son. "I…uh, I don't know what to say. That's so admirable."

"Admirable?" Bonnie laughed. "I don't know about that. It's just what I do to pay the bills."

Charlie ran back in with picture in hand. "Here's my daddy."

She took the picture from him. A Hispanic young man with wavy black hair was holding a tiny boy. The expression on his face showed how much he loved the little baby in his arms. "Oh, he's very handsome. Just like you."

She flipped the picture over. In a scribbled handwriting, it said Carlos II and III.

Charlie giggled. "That's me he's holding."

"Very nice." She needed to talk with Nate. If he hadn't already called, she needed to convince him not to. Angelina might not know the whole story, but this woman loved her son. She had the right to decide where she wanted to live. Angelina stood. "It was so nice to meet you, Mrs. Wright. Now, I see why Charlie is such a good kid. He has a good mother."

The woman's face flushed with pleasure. "Thank you. That is so nice of you to say. Please come back again."

~*~

"It's too late." Nate stared at Angelina.

"What do you mean it's too late? I'm telling you this woman didn't commit a crime. She loves her son, and he loves her. She works hard to make sure he has a nice place to live. If she doesn't want to live near her family, doesn't she have that right?"

"Of course she has that right, but I already contacted the sheriff's department in California. The police department will verify she's safe and not missing, and then report that back to whoever filed the report in the first place. While I'd love to pursue this, we have to be careful of jurisdiction."

Nate was probably right. It didn't sound like a big deal, but something still felt wrong. "Can you check out her story about her husband dying?"

"Probably, what was his name again?"

"Carlos Perez II."

Nate's fingers clicked on the keyboard. "Yep. A Carlos Perez was killed in a car accident about four years ago in that area of California, so it sounds as though she was telling the truth. The obituary lists his wife as Bonnie, and a son, Carlos III."

"So she did tell me the truth. I bet she went back to using her maiden name. But why is Charlie using it as well?"

"And why he's going by Charles and not Carlos." Nate added.

"Is that against the law? To change your name like that?"

He shrugged. "I'm sure it happens. As long as she's using the correct social security number, it's not a problem. I guess if she wants to Anglicize his name from Carlos to Charles, that's her prerogative."

"So she probably hasn't done anything wrong, right?"

"Right. But I do need to talk with her and verify she is that Bonita Wright Perez and have her contact the sheriff in that county."

"I thought you already did that."

"I did, but they asked me to verify the info so they can take her off the missing persons list."

"So who put her on the list anyway?"

"The deputy I talked with didn't actually tell me."

"It would be interesting to find out."

"Why?"

She shrugged. "I don't know. What if she doesn't want to be found? It seems to me she's made some effort to make it more difficult. She's changed their names somewhat, and apparently, she's not in contact with them."

"True. But what if it's all a big misunderstanding? Things can get quite emotional after the death of a loved one and things can be said and done that everyone regrets. Maybe the person who reported them missing just wants to reconnect with them."

"I suppose."

20

What if? What if? Angelina's mind had come up with scenario after scenario about why Bonnie left her home without telling anyone, and why she didn't want to be found. And most of them weren't happy scenarios. Her own curiosity could have put into motion events that could hurt Charlie.

She should have never gotten involved.

They were doing just fine until she put her nose where it didn't belong in their business. Angelina sat in her car. She picked up the phone and pressed the phone icon. "Keren, I'm...uh, sorry. Something came up so I can't go to dinner tonight after all."

"What's wrong? Are you OK?"

Angelina shook her head. Keren acted more and more like her mother every day. "I'm fine. I just have something I need to do. Something important. I'll tell you all about it later."

"What?"

"Nothing to concern yourself with."

"Oh...sorry I didn't mean to interfere." Angelina could hear the hurt in Keren's voice. "Not a problem. I guess we can eat pancakes and sausage for dinner."

Angelina ignored her tone. "That sounds yummy. And don't forget to tell Peter we'll have a talk tomorrow about becoming the groundskeeper for the estate."

"That really isn't—"

"I'm not having that argument again. See you tomorrow." She clicked her phone off as she headed out of town. Angelina drove down the rural road once again. She'd tell Bonnie the truth so that she'd at least not be in complete shock when Nate talked with her the next day.

A black SUV sat in the driveway.

Bonnie's car had been an old green hatchback that had seen better days. Oh well, maybe a friend was watching Charlie while Bonnie worked.

She pulled in behind the car. Before she could step out, both doors on the SUV opened.

The man on the driver's side walked to her car while the other simply stood and glared at her.

Angelina's pulse spiked.

They didn't seem like nice people. The expression on their faces was anything but friendly. Angelina couldn't help but notice the size of the man walking toward her. She clicked the locks on all her doors.

He rapped on the window as he leaned toward her. "I need to talk to you."

Her palms moistened. "About what?"

"About the people who live in this house."

"What about them?"

"Open the door. I can't hear you."

Yeah, right. That wasn't likely. Instead she rolled the window down—a few inches. "Can you hear me now?"

"Who are you?" The man asked as he leaned down to get a better look.

"Why?"

"Excuse me?"

"I said why do you want to know who I am?"

"I'm with the FBI."

Angelina stared. He didn't seem like FBI to her. "And we're looking for the people who live here. That's why. And if you know where they are, we need to know."

"Let's see your badge."

He smiled, more like a grimace. "It's in the car, but I can assure you I'm FBI."

Probably not. "Why does the FBI want them?"

"It's a private matter. So where are they?"

"How would I know? I...I just pulled in the drive to turn around."

"So you don't know them?"

"Not really."

"That sounds like you do know them." His dark brown eyes glared.

"Like I said, not really. I've met her once. I was just turning around in their drive."

"So you said, but—"

"Gotta go. Bye." Angelina forced a smile and waved her fingers at him as she put her car into reverse.

The man stared after her as she pulled out.

If those men were the FBI, she was the pope. But who were they, and why were they looking for Bonnie and Charlie?

Her phone alerted to an incoming text message. Unusual, these days. Only a few people even had her new number. She picked it up off the passenger seat. A text message from Nate. She pulled off the side of the road. She retrieved the text.

911! MEET ME AT YOUR HOUSE.

That sounded serious. If Nate needed her, she'd do whatever she could to help him. She owed him that and more. He'd been there for her time and time again.

Day was becoming night when she pulled into her drive ten minutes later. Nate's car sat in front of the garage. He was leaning against his car as he waited for her. She pulled up beside him. After shutting off her car, she stepped out of it. "What's wrong? Why did you 911 me? Are you all right?"

"I think I made a mistake. A big mistake." He shook his head.

"What do you mean? What are you talking about?"

"I called the sheriff's department again. I talked to another deputy who knew more about Bonita and Carlos Perez." He stopped talking as if gathering his thoughts.

"And…"

"And he explained the whole situation to me."

"That doesn't sound—"

"Is there a problem?" Keren yelled as she half-ran, half-walked across the lawn toward them.

Angelina jumped at the sound of her voice. "Stop sneaking up on me, Keren. You know I hate that. Especially in the dark."

"I wasn't sneaking, and it isn't dark yet. I simply opened the door and walked out. You were just too busy to notice." She glanced at Nate. "What's going on? Are you arresting her?"

Nate smiled. "Just having a conversation with Angelina."

"It looked pretty intense." Keren's voice was doubtful. "I saw you when you pulled up but you didn't come up to the house. So I assumed you were waiting for Angelina. Where were you anyway, Angelina? I was—"

"Worried." Angelina finished her cousin's

sentence. "Keren, I love you more than you can imagine, but it's not your job to worry about me every moment I'm away from you. And nothing is wrong." That might not be exactly true. "At least nothing you need to worry about."

Peter walked across the lawn. "Hey, what's going on?"

Nate looked at Angelina.

Peter looped an arm around Keren's shoulder, his concern very real. "What's going on?"

Angelina smiled. "Nate and I are talking. We had a situation come up at the school, and we decided to discuss in private the best way to handle it. See you later."

"But—"

"No buts. It's between us. Nothing more. I promise a rain check on dinner." She grabbed Nate by the arm and propelled him toward the garage.

"I wasn't trying to barge in. I was only worried about you." Keren called after her, her tone sounding hurt.

Angelina turned back. "And I love you for that, Keren, but Nate and I need to talk about this. Alone. See you tomorrow." Once they were inside the garage, she turned to Nate. "What's the problem?"

They sat down on the steps leading up to her apartment.

"The deputy...let me just start at the beginning. Apparently, Carlos II's family is very rich. There's some speculation they might be involved in the drug trade in Mexico, but no one knows that for sure. Anyway, little Charlie's father's family wanted little Carlos to live with them after the death of their son. I guess Bonnie got tired of them interfering and left."

"That's awful. I should have just stayed out of it." She put her hands in her head. "Now they'll find out she lives here and will start bothering her again. This is all my fault. I never—"

"Don't say that because it's not true. You only had Charlie's best interests in mind when you started asking a few questions. In fact, you're the one who told me to slow down. I should have talked with her first." His hand rubbed her back.

"I'm the one who got you involved. It's my fault."

He moved his hand away as he stood. "Well, it's done now. I need to tell her what's going on so she won't be completely shocked if her deceased husband's family comes visiting soon. And my guess would be very soon after what I heard."

"Yeah, that's what I thought, too, so I went to her house." The men in the black SUV. Charlie's family already? "Oh, no."

"Oh, no, what?"

"When I went there, there were two men in a car there waiting for her. He said he was FBI, but when I asked for his ID, he said it was in the car. And they were sort of scary. But it couldn't be the father's family. How would they have gotten here that quick?"

"Rich people have their ways. You should know that. Maybe I should call her."

"I don't think she's home. The lights were off. She told me she cleans some offices in the evening for extra money and that Charlie–Carlos goes with her."

"Which one?"

She searched her mind. "I can't remember. Sorry."

"Maybe we can find her before she goes back home so she knows what's going on. That way she won't be shocked if the men in the SUV are still there."

Angelina looked at Nate. "You said the family might be involved with drugs. You don't think they'd hurt Bonnie to get Charlie?"

Nate met her gaze. "Anything's possible."

21

Angelina fought the urge to bite a fingernail as they drove from office building to office building searching for Bonnie Wright-Perez. Why couldn't she remember the name of the building? She was sure Bonnie had said it.

Nate turned down an alley. "There's another office down here. I don't know what else we can do except go to her house and wait for her. Which might be a good idea, anyway. I think I'd like to talk to the men in the SUV." Nate's phone rang. When he looked at the screen, he told her, "The station." He slowed the car to a stop then clicked the answer icon. "Nate Goodman." He put it on speaker.

"Chief, I got an FBI agent here who's insisting he has to talk to you."

"Put him on."

"Goodman, this is Agent Eugene Jackson from the Cleveland office. We need to talk. How soon can you meet me at the station?"

"About what?"

"I'll explain when you get here. When will that be?"

Nate looked at Angelina.

She shrugged.

"Be there in ten minutes or so." He looked at Angelina. "Probably more like fifteen."

"I'll be waiting."

Nate hung up and looked at Angelina. "I wonder what that's about. Maybe the guys in the SUV really were FBI. I'll drive you back to your house first."

"Good. I'll get my car and keep looking for her."

"I don't like that idea."

"Why not?"

"It might not be safe. If those men at her house really were sent from the Perez family and not FBI, we have no idea how far they'll go to get back their employer's grandchild."

~*~

Nate parked his car and walked into the station. A man was pacing at the other end of the room. He was African-American and bald. Not the description of the either man Angelina had encountered. It looked as if he were talking—more like ranting—to someone. He would pace one way and then the other. His hands never stopped moving. Nate wasn't about to let the FBI come in and bully his officers, no matter the reason. Nate hurried into the station.

He'd stopped pacing by the time Nate reached him. "Agent Jackson? I'm Nate Goodman. How can I help you?"

The two men shook hands.

"It's more a case of us helping you."

"We might have a problem." Leslie gave a little wave as she stepped around Agent Jackson.

"Leslie, what are you doing here?"

"Where else would I be when there's a problem in my old stomping grounds?" Her voice held a hint of pleasure that she'd been able to shock him. "Nice to see you, Nate."

"Always nice to see you, too. Why is the FBI here?"

"Because we have a situation," Jackson said.

"And what would that be?"

"The Bonita and Carlos Perez situation," Leslie said.

His stomach twisted. "I didn't know it was a situation. What's the problem?"

"We received a tip about a plan to kidnap Carlos Perez and take him to Mexico."

His worst fear became a reality. His one little phone call had put them in danger—and now Angelina as well. "Maybe you should tell me the whole story."

"It seems when little Carlos the Third's father died, the father's parents were devastated. They wanted the chance to raise their grandchild as their own. Thus, they wanted to take the child to Mexico where they can raise him without interference from the mother or the United States government."

"How reliable is the tip?"

"Very. It came from a trusted employee who overheard the plan and decided they couldn't be a part of such a scheme so they called us. The last we heard was that the Perez family have feet on the ground here in Ohio. That means we need to find them before Perez's people do."

Hoping he was wrong, he asked, "Do you have men waiting at their house in a black SUV?"

"No, why do you ask?"

"I heard there were two men looking for them there."

"From whom?" Leslie asked.

There was no reason to bring Angelina's name in the discussion. "Do you think they're dangerous?"

"If they're from the Perez family, very much so."

~*~

Angelina pulled into the alley behind the Simpson law offices. She'd finally remembered the name. A car pulled in from the other direction at the same time. A dark SUV.

Quickly, she shut off her car lights, hoping they hadn't noticed her.

Two men stepped out from both sides of the car. The same men she'd seen earlier. How had they found Bonnie? Probably talked to a neighbor. If only she'd remembered the name earlier, they'd be long gone by now.

The men walked over to Bonnie's old green car.

She needed to get Charlie and his mom out of there before the men found them.

Her cell phone buzzed. It was Nate, but she had no time to talk now.

She shut off the phone and stepped out of the car. Using the bushes to hide, she crept along the alley as the darkness crowded in. Being in the dark had never bothered her before Luther Marks. Now it terrified her. Nothing good ever happened in the dark. Her trembling body wanted to give in to the fear—to hyperventilate, but she refused. Noisy breathing would bring attention to the fact she was sneaking down the alley. Besides, if she breathed too loudly she might wake up sleeping dogs. A bunch of barking dogs would announce that she was there.

She stumbled on an unseen root and toppled to the ground. She held her breath, sure the men would rush to where she was. One of the men glanced her way but didn't move. She held her breath and waited. One…two…three…When she was convinced they weren't coming after her, she stood and peered through the branches.

The men were talking. The one nodded to the other and walked toward the building.

Time to get moving. She moved past the cars until she was even with the side of the building. The glare of the lights from the windows brought some comfort.

The man by the car was on the phone, his back to her. The other was at the door. She took a deep breath, left the safety the bushes provided and ran to the side of the building. She listened. Apparently, neither man noticed her. So far–so good. Quietly she made her way down the side of the building. She peeked into each window as she passed.

The man began pounding on the door and yelled, "Fire. Fire. Is anybody in here? You need to get out of the building. Fire!"

That was sure to get Bonnie's attention.

Angelina picked up her pace, hurrying from window to window. Finally. At the fourth window Bonnie stood in the middle of the room holding a trashcan, but her attention was focused on the door. She obviously could hear the men yelling and was probably wondering what to do.

Angelina rapped against the window.

Bonnie jumped then turned toward her. Her eyes grew wide when she recognized Angelina. Angelina shook her head, put a finger to her mouth in a shushing gesture, and then mouthed the words—*I need to talk to you. Right now.*

The pounding and screaming at the door continued.

Bonnie looked at her then back at the door. She seemed frozen.

Angelina motioned for her to come to the window. A moment later, the window opened.

"I know this is crazy, but I don't have time to explain. We need to get out of here. Right now. Where's Carlos?" Angelina used an urgent tone.

Bonnie gasped. "My son's name is Charlie. Not Carlos."

"We don't have time to play games. We've got to get out of here. Right now. There's no fire. Those men are here to find you. Trust me. I want to help you and Carlos."

She blinked and then nodded. She called out, "Char—"

"Momma. Those men said there's a fire. We better get out—"

"Charlie. Come here now. We have to go." Bonnie motioned toward Angelina at the window.

His eyes grew wide. "Miss Angelina."

"Hush now. We have to go with Miss Angelina. Right now." Without a moment's hesitation, Bonnie hefted Charlie through the window into Angelina's arms. A moment later, Bonnie climbed through the window.

"This way." Grabbing each of their hands Angelina led them to the bushes. Once hidden, she whispered, "We need to be quiet. My car's this way."

When the parking lot came into view, Bonnie stopped moving. Angelina tugged on her hand to urge her forward.

One man now stood beside Bonnie's car, but his attention was on the building and his partner. Slowly, they moved past him. He yelled at the other. "Just break a window. Let's get the kid and go. Before someone calls the cops. We're making too much noise."

The shattering of glass echoed through the darkness. Angelina tugged again, Bonnie seemed frozen in fear. They had to get to the car before the men realized they weren't in the building. Finally, the darkened shape of her car came into view.

She leaned toward Bonnie and whispered, "Get in the back and duck down."

Angelina ran to the driver's side and opened the door. The moment she was in the car, she hit the lock buttons. Behind her Bonnie and Charlie hid on the floor. A moment later the car roared to life.

The man turned toward them He yelled at the other man. "Get the car."

Angelina slammed the car in reverse and hit the gas. Her own nerves were getting the best of her, but she'd fall apart later. Right now, she had to get Charlie and Bonnie away from these men. She held her breath as they careened down the alley—backward.

The SUV barreled toward them.

Angelina hit the brake long enough to move the gear into drive. Then her foot pressed down—hard—and they surged forward out of sight of the SUV.

Seconds later, lights from the other vehicle entered the street.

"Where are we going?" Bonnie asked.

"Away from them."

"I'm scared, Mama." Charlie's voice trembled.

So was Angelina, but she couldn't tell them that.

She'd made this mess and she needed to fix it. She yelled back, "Don't be scared, Charlie. Just a little adventure like in the book, *Where the Wild Things Are*."

"That was pretend. This is real."

Angelina had to agree with that—very real. She looked in the rearview mirror. The SUV was gaining on them. "We've got the get away from them so we can go back to my house. Until we can figure out what to do."

The SUV slammed into her back bumper.

She struggled with the wheel. The moment she felt back in control, she hit the gas and surged away from them. At the next street she turned left. The car fishtailed but kept moving forward. At the next street she made another turn and then another.

The SUV was still behind them but was losing ground.

She made another turn and then shut the lights off as she quickly turned into another alley then quickly did several more turns. She looked over at Bonnie.

Charlie was clutching his mother and crying. Bonnie was wiping tears from her own face but was doing her best to calm him down. "It's OK, sweetie."

"I think we lost them."

Bonnie looked behind them. After a few moments, she said, "I think you're right. I don't see them."

"Good. We can go to my house."

They drove in silence.

If Keren or Peter saw them, they'd start asking questions. Keren, the mother hen, would probably be watching out the window if she heard Angelina's car. Knowing her, she might even come out to the car to check on Angelina so she pulled the car to the side of the road. "I'll drop you off here. Then you'll need to walk to the back of that building so nobody sees you."

"Why can't they see us?" Charlie–Carlos asked.

"Hush now, Charlie. We've talked about this before. You know it's important for nobody to know our real names. It's the same thing now. We need to do exactly what Miss Angelina says. She's helping us."

"OK, Mama."

"Thank you, sweetie. We'll talk about all this soon. Very soon. But not right now."

"Yes, Mama." His voice was filled with complete trust for his mother. Charlie obviously knew she would never do anything to hurt him.

What must it be like to have that sort of trust? She thought of Nate. Did she trust him that much? She did. "Walk to the back of the garage. That building there. I'll let you in as soon as I get there."

Bonnie was already getting out of her side. She leaned in to pick Charlie up.

"No. Mama. I'm a big boy I can walk by myself."

A glance at the main house showed no lights. Of course, that didn't mean Keren wasn't up and peeking out. But there was no way she could see Charlie or Bonnie behind the garage.

Angelina pushed the button for the garage door. She drove in and quickly hit the close button. A minute later she was opening the back door of the garage. "Be careful, it's dark in here. I don't want to turn the light on. We'll talk in a minute," Angelina said to her guests.

No one spoke as the three of them made their way up the darkened steps.

She opened the door, herded Bonnie and Charlie inside and turned on the light. She locked the door and finally took a deep breath. She leaned against the door, trying to gather her wits. Then she forced a smile and turned toward Bonnie and Charlie.

They both looked confused—and scared. And why wouldn't they? "Bonita, do you want me to talk in front of Carlos?"

"Please call us Bonnie and Charlie. Those are our names now. Right, Charlie?"

"Right, Mama."

Bonnie leaned down and hugged Charlie then looked over at Angelina. "He's probably tired. It's way past his bedtime. I had to work a little later than normal." She took a deep breath "Do you have a place for Charlie to sleep and then we can talk?"

"Of course." Angelina walked over to her bedroom door and opened it. "He can sleep in here."

Several minutes later Bonnie walked out of the room wiping away the tears.

"I'm so sorry about all of this." Angelina gave her a quick hug. "I know this has been terrifying. Do you know those men who followed us?"

"Not them, but I know men like them and I know who sent them."

"Who?"

"Charlie's grandparents. On his father's side. They are very rich and powerful people in Mexico. They are used to getting what they want, and they want my son."

"Oh."

"My husband walked away from his family, their nasty little business, and their money. As much as they didn't like it, they allowed him to do that. We were happy and living our own life in California, but when Carlos died everything changed."

"I can imagine." Angelina motioned at a chair.

Bonnie sat down. "At first, they were nice to me

after my husband's death, but they kept trying to get me to come to Mexico. For a visit, they said. But I knew enough about them to not trust them. They became more insistent, and that's when I decided to leave. But I don't understand how they found us. I've tried to be so careful."

"My fault. I messed everything up. Something bothered me about Charlie so I went to my friend. He's the Chief of Police and one thing led to another, and we found out you were listed as missing. He called the Sheriff's Department in California and I guess they contacted them." Angelina took a breath. "I am so sorry."

Bonnie sat down. Her head drooped. "I just...I can't let them take my boy from me. He..." She looked up at Angelina. "He's my everything. When I wouldn't go to Mexico, they made up lies about me and said a judge would give them custody. Before it got to that point, I left. I couldn't take the chance."

"I can help you disappear again."

She nodded.

"But I don't think it's the best way. You don't really want to live like this for the rest of your lives, do you? Hiding out and running."

"I will if it means I can raise my son. I don't care how hard it is." Her voice was fierce. "He's my son. I can't let those people have him."

"What if we can find a better way?"

"What do you mean?"

"I'm not sure, but there has to be a way for you and Charlie to be free to live your lives. We just have to figure out what. The government won't let them come and take Charlie. He's an American citizen."

"I'm not sure they care about American law." Her

head drooped once more. "But I'm so tired of running. I want my son to have a normal life. Do you think that's even possible?"

22

Nate walked up to Bonnie Wright-Perez's car while Leslie walked toward the building.

"Looks like a break-in. We've got broken glass over here," Leslie called.

Nate and Agent Jackson walked over.

"It looks as if we're too late. They got here first." Jackson was glum.

Nate's stomach twisted. "You think they've kidnapped the boy?"

"Unless they got away. Which isn't very likely. Wonder how they knew where she was?" Jackson looked down at the broken glass.

"It wouldn't be all that hard, Eugene. All they'd had to do was ask a neighbor. Most people in Mt. Pleasant are too nice. They'd just tell them what they wanted to know to be helpful." Leslie sounded irritated.

"Being nice is usually considered a good thing, Leslie." Nate was reminded how truly different the two of them were.

"Not in this case." She stalked off to the side of the building. A moment later, she called, "Found something!"

Nate and Agent Jackson met her at the side.

Leslie stood by a window. "All the rooms are empty but this window isn't completely closed and the lights are still on. As you can see."

"Maybe they got out." Nate suggested—hoped. Could Angelina have found them in time? He started to open the window.

Leslie grabbed his arm. "Don't touch it. We need to get fingerprints." She motioned at the ledge. "The ledge and the window."

"Why would we need to do that?" Nate asked.

"I'm hoping she was here cleaning when someone showed up at the door and scared her. And then she climbed out the window to get away. Of course, it could be that someone else came in through the window and she didn't get away at all. That's why we need the fingerprints. To see who actually touched this windowsill."

"Got a fingerprint kit?" Jackson asked.

"In my trunk."

After a search of the building showed it to be empty and the fingerprints were taken they headed back to the station. He left one officer behind on the off-chance that Bonnie Wright- Perez showed up again.

Nate kept dialing Angelina, but she wasn't answering. His memory kept going to the night he'd rescued her. She'd come back for him, saved him from being killed. Had she overcome her fear of the dark to try to help Bonnie and Charlie? Something told him it was possible, but it was also possible the bad guys had all of them—even Angelina. *Please God, keep them safe.*

Once at the station, Leslie took over as if she were still the chief.

Nate said nothing as she processed the prints and began running them through databases.

His mind was on Angelina. Where was she and why wasn't she answering her phone?

Two night officers milled around, obviously not

sure what to make of what was happening. Mt. Pleasant was usually a quiet town, the odd drunk, teenaged shenanigans and other petty crimes.

"This is as good a time to ask if any of them know or have been in contact with Bonnie Perez."

"Go for it."

Eugene walked to the middle of the room. "Listen up. I'm wondering if either of you know Bonnie and Charles Wright."

One officer stepped forward. "They come to our church once in a while, but I can't say I know them very well."

"Do you have a number we can call? She has no idea what kind of danger she's in. We need to make contact with her as soon as possible."

"I only know them to say hello."

A female officer stepped forward. "Her son is in my daughter's class at school, but I don't have a number for her either. I could probably call Miss Dawkins, their teacher. She might have a number."

"Do that, please."

She nodded and walked to a desk.

"You won't believe this, Nate." Leslie stormed out of his office. "The fingerprints belong to—"

"Angelina Matthews." He finished the sentence for Leslie. "That's good. That means Angelina might have found them before the bad guys. So they could all be safe."

"Or they could all be in trouble. Serious trouble." Leslie glared at him. "You've been holding out on us. What does Angelina have to do with any of this? How'd she get involved? And why didn't you tell us about her before?"

"She's the reason I checked Charlie's prints in the

first place. Which is how I found out they were listed as missing. But the last I saw of Angelina she was at her house. I've been trying to get in contact with her, but she's not answering her phone."

"So I guess you and the famous Ange are an item now?"

"We're friends, Les—"

Eugene gave Leslie a warning look. "I don't really care what any of you are. I want her found so we can find out what's going on."

The door opened.

Angelina walked in.

"Well, if it isn't Ange Matthews," Leslie said, her tone still irritated.

"I go by Angelina now."

"Where are they?" Eugene Jackson walked up to Angelina. "Do you have them? The Perezes?"

Meeting his gaze, Angelina smiled. "In a safe place."

"I hope you're right about that," Leslie muttered.

"But there are two men after them. We heard them say they wanted Charlie." She looked at Nate. "They're the same men I saw earlier at their house."

"What kind of car?" Leslie asked,

"A black SUV."

"I don't suppose you got a license number?" Leslie jeered.

Angelina gave her a look then answered, "I was a little busy trying to get away from them. So, no, I didn't."

Leslie turned away from Angelina, obviously frustrated.

Jackson looked at Nate. "Can your people go look for the SUV?"

Nate nodded and walked over to his waiting officers.

"This is a mess," Angelina said as she came up to Nate. "And it's all my fault. I should have minded my own business. According to Bonnie, the grandparents can be quite ruthless. She indicated they're involved in drugs."

Nate touched her arm. "It's not your fault. Let's all go in my office. See if we can figure something out."

Leslie walked in and sat behind the desk—his desk.

"You're in my seat, Leslie."

Her face flushed red, but she stood and moved to an empty seat beside Angelina. After he sat, Nate looked at Eugene Jackson. "What's your plan?"

"First we need to make sure they're safe." Eugene nodded then looked at Angelina. "Are you sure they're safe?"

"I think so. I mean why wouldn't they be safe at my house? Certainly, those men have no reason to go to my house looking for them." She looked at Nate. "Right?"

He nodded. "Tell us what happened tonight at the law offices."

Angelina explained it all in short, concise sentences.

"Well those men are probably out there right now," Leslie said. "I doubt very much they just gave up and drove away. Are you sure they didn't follow you back to your house?"

"As sure as I can be."

"I hope you're right. But they could have gotten your license number and had someone get your address so maybe they aren't as safe as you thought."

"Not true. The car I used was my father's. It hasn't even been registered in years."

"Oh so you admit you committed a crime?" Leslie arched a brow.

"Don't be ridiculous, Leslie." Eugene's tone said he wasn't in the mood for joking."

"Sorry, just trying to lighten the mood." Leslie gave an insincere smile. She turned to Eugene. "What are we going to do to keep them safe?"

"I've been thinking about that." Angelina looked at Nate. "I have an idea. What if we call the sheriff's office in California and tell them it wasn't Carlos and Bonita Perez at all, but a case of wrong identity. Not the people they were looking for. Maybe they'd just go away and leave them alone."

Leslie fluffed her hair. "That's awfully simplistic. I don't think it would work."

Eugene spoke up. "I'm not so sure about that, Leslie. It could be enough to call off the Perez family's dogs."

Leslie's face turned red. "I don't think it will work."

"And they wouldn't have to go on the run again. They could stay here." Nate smiled at Angelina. "I think it's a brilliant idea, Angelina."

"It sounds way too easy." Leslie glared at Angelina.

Leslie always wanted to be the one to come up with the idea. Apparently, she hadn't changed. And it was obvious that she didn't like Angelina.

"Sometimes easy is the best way." Nate reached for his phone. "Let me give them a call and see what happens."

The others listened as he talked to a deputy.

Nate hung up. "I think that's all we can do for now. Everyone might as well call it a night. I'll go to Angelina's to keep everyone safe. Hopefully, my officers will find the black SUV before long. And we can get them behind bars so they can't hurt anyone."

"I think it would be better if they didn't get arrested here in Mt. Pleasant. We don't want to give them a reason to hang around."

The phone rang.

"What are the chances this is the Perez family or one of their minions?" Nate asked.

"Probably pretty good." Eugene said. "Want me to handle this?"

"Sure." Nate motioned at the phone.

Eugene picked up the phone and identified himself. "I'm very sorry to have gotten your hopes up, Senor Perez, but it was a definite wrong identification. You know how small-town cops can be." He grinned at Nate. "They jumped the gun on this thing."

He listened, and then responded. "Yep. I came down right away to check out the situation for myself. I can tell you unequivocally, the people in question are not the ones you're looking for. It was all just a big mix-up. Again, I'm so sorry for getting your hopes up, but there was an incident tonight. I was wondering if you or your employees had anything to do with a break-in at the building where this Bonnie woman worked."

Nate gave a thumbs-up to Eugene.

"Because we would take a very dim view if you were involved in the break-in." Eugene listened for a moment. "Of course, I'm sure you're right. It probably was just a coincidence. Again, my apologies for the mix-up."

He hung up and looked at the group. "Well, they sounded convinced. I think we've got the situation under control. I suggest the Wrights stay away from their house for a few days. Or even better, they find a new home. As far as we know, the goons never saw them. And I'd like to keep it that way."

"I can take care of that," Angelina said.

"Of course you can," Leslie replied.

Eugene nodded. "And about the two goons. I think we should let them get on their way without an arrest. The less they have to do with this town, the safer Bonita and Carlos will be."

"Good idea, Agent Jackson," Nate said.

Leslie, are you ready to go?"

"I'll be there in a second. I need to—"

Nate's cell phone rang. "Nate here."

"Chief, we just drove past the Wright house. The SUV's in the drive. Want us to talk to them?"

Nate thought for a moment. "No, just watch them. If they leave, follow them to see where they're going." After he hung up, he looked at the others. "If I'm right, they'll be leaving in a few minutes, and we can put this all to bed. And bed sounds like a good idea. I'm going home. It's been a long day."

"Nate, we need to talk." Leslie put a hand on his arm.

"Leslie, I'm exhausted, and I'm going home. Angelina, do you need a ride?"

"Not too tired to drive her home though, huh?" Leslie sniped.

Nate smiled at Leslie. "You can call me tomorrow if you want to talk about this situation. Just not too early. I'll be sleeping in. How about it, Angelina? Need that ride?"

"No, thanks. I have my car. I'm so sorry about this whole mess, Nate. Really."

"There's nothing to apologize for. If I don't see you before, I'll see you at the next meeting. Right?"

Leslie didn't move. "I want to talk to you, Nate. And I'm not leaving until I do."

"I'll let the two of you talk in private." Angelina turned to leave.

"That's not necessary." His phone rang. He punched a button. "Nate here." He listened, and then hung up. "The SUV pulled out of the drive. My officers followed them to the county line. Guess they're leaving so…all's well that ends well."

"Are you going to talk to me, Nate?"

Some things couldn't be avoided and apparently Leslie was one of those things. "Sure. What do you want to talk about?"

"About us."

"There is no us. But there's no hard feelings. I think you were right to break off the engagement."

Leslie bit her lips. "I'm not so sure. I think we can work it out."

Something he had no interest in doing, but he didn't want to be mean about it. "That's sweet. But both of us know we're just too different to make that happen. I wish you the best. I really do."

"I guess this has to do with Angelina."

"God bless you, Leslie. I hope you find what you're looking for." He knew he had, but he wasn't going to get into that with her. Instead, he moved forward and hugged her. Out of the corner of his eye, he saw Angelina watching. She turned and walked out of the station.

23

Twenty minutes until the meeting started.

Angelina stared at the clock. She had no intention of going to that meeting. She'd promised Dr. Markley to give it a try and she had. Much to her surprise the meetings had been helpful, but after the last one, she was done...finished. The humiliation of the anxiety attack was one she could live without.

Besides they all knew who she was now, and they'd treat her differently anyway so what was the point of even going. Not to mention, she didn't need to complicate Nate's life. Leslie still seemed quite interested in Nate. And after the hug she'd seen last night, it looked as if Nate might fell the same way. Nope, the best thing she could do was to stay out of the way. She'd miss him, but...

Her gaze strayed back to the clock.

Eighteen minutes.

A part of her wanted to go. Maybe Rosie went on another date. Perhaps Fred liked his new job. And it might be that Max finished his book—if there actually was a book. Another glance at the clock.

Sixtee—

A knock on the door made her jump. Must be Keren. Worried that she wasn't capable of fixing something to eat when she got hungry. Which reminded Angelina that she needed to buy some cookbooks or maybe watch how-to videos. She walked over and opened the door.

"Evening, Angelina." Nate grinned.

"What are you doing here?"

"I thought we could drive to the meeting together."

"I'm not going."

"I was afraid you'd feel like that. That's why I stopped. You really have nothing to be embarrassed about. It was a small anxiety attack. I've seen worse. Actually, I've had worse ones myself."

"I just…after what happened, I can't."

"It's really important for you to come tonight."

"Why?"

"It's all about the getting back on the horse thing. If you don't want to come back after tonight, fine with me. But you've gotta come back tonight, or you're giving in to the PTSD. And if you do that, Luther wins. You don't want that, do you?" He grinned again.

"I know, but still…"

The seconds ticked by.

"So, are you ready to go?"

She shook her head. "I…I can't."

"Of course, you can. You're not the only one with anxiety attacks. You can't let one little panic attack stop you from going to the meeting."

"Why not?"

"Now don't go reading more into this than you should. The truth is that I'd hate to be the reason you quit. In fact, if you quit, I'll have to assume it was my fault. And that could cause me to have my own setback. Do you want to be the reason I have a setback?"

"You won't have a setback, and you know it."

"It could happen, and I know you wouldn't want

to be the cause. Would you?"

"You're impossible to say no to, but you already know that, right?"

He shrugged.

"Yoo-hoo." Keren walked up the steps. "Oh, I didn't know you had company."

Nate smiled. "Just thought I'd see if Angelina wanted a ride to the meeting tonight."

"If she needs a ride to the meeting, I'll be glad to take her."

Why did everyone think she was so incompetent that she couldn't even get herself to a meeting? She took a deep breath, fought off the floating sensation that threatened, and fanned the tiny spark of outrage that they were treating her like a child.

Both of them were looking at her.

"Are you all right?" Keren asked. "You look a little pale."

She nodded. "I'm fine. Nate, that was very nice of you to stop, but I can drive myself." She walked into her apartment and picked up her purse and keys. She smiled at the two of them. "See you later, Keren. Nate, I'll be right behind you."

Nate winked. "Sounds like a plan."

"Are you sure you don't need me to drive you?" Keren asked.

"I'm quite capable of driving myself to the meeting."

"I know that." Keren smiled. "Have a good meeting."

Nate walked down the steps ahead of them, whistling.

Keren followed behind as Angelina made her way to her car.

He was already in his car and driving away.

"Angelina."

She turned to her cousin. "What?"

"I'm a little worried about you."

"Why?"

"I think you're doing too much too soon. Dr. Markley said to take baby steps. But you're running here and there. Trying to do everything at once. And after all that happened with that little boy and his mother, I worry that it's been too much stress for you. I don't want you to get sick again."

"I'm fine."

"And I know something's going on between you and that policeman. He keeps coming here all the time. Why don't you just tell him to leave you alone?"

"He's not bothering me. We're friends."

"Fine. If you say so." Keren hugged her. "All I'm saying is don't do too much too soon. You're not as strong as you think you are."

Angelina got in her car and drove away.

You're not as strong as you think you are. You're not as strong as you think you are. You're not...

"Shut up." She screamed to the empty car. But that was the truth. She wasn't strong enough. Certainly not good enough for Nate. He deserved a healthy person. Not someone like her. Her parents would be so disappointed in her. That was her truth.

Luther had told her that over and over.

Keren, who loved her, was even telling her that.

"It's not true. You're wrong. You're wrong. I am..." She stopped, unable to say the words. "Get hold of yourself, Angelina." She didn't need to have another anxiety attack at the meeting.

She pulled into the church parking lot.

Nate's car was there, but he must have gone in without her.

Oh, well...she was strong enough to walk into that room alone. There she'd said the word. Alone. That was a start. Nate was right. They wouldn't judge her. They'd all been through their own bad times. Jumping out of her car, she hurried into the church.

"Are you mad at me?"

She jumped. "Where did you come from?"

"I was waiting for you."

"Well, stop it. You scared me." She was pleased that he'd waited.

"Sorry. So are you mad at me? Because you seemed sort of irritated at me when I left. Not to mention you left the station last night without saying good-bye."

"I didn't want to interrupt your conversation with Leslie."

"That's all done with, Angelina."

"It didn't look done to me. That hug looked quite friendly."

"It was a good-bye hug. I am not interested in Leslie. At all."

Angelina fought back the desire to cheer. "Besides, the only person I'm irritated at is me. I am so sick of myself."

"You need to cut yourself a break. You went through a lot. And you're getting stronger every day. I think you're quite amazing actually."

"That's not true. I almost had an anxiety attack on the way over here."

"Key word. Almost. We each have our own journey to take."

"I don't feel like I'm making any progress with

mine."

"Are you kidding me? Look at what you accomplished in the past few days. You actually figured out a way to keep Charlie safe. So I really don't know how you can say that."

"Because it's true. I only did what I did because I messed up in the first place. Luther's right, my life is pitiful and worthless."

"Luther isn't right about anything. He's dead. Remember?" His gaze met hers.

"You know what I meant." She walked away and then turned back. "Come on. We're late. And that's not good since you're the leader. And no, I'm not mad at you."

"Glad to hear that because that would make me sad." He took hold of her arm as his gaze locked with hers.

She couldn't breathe.

Nate moved closer. "I know this isn't the right time."

"For what?"

"For us, but…" He leaned close. His lips met hers.

She closed her eyes savoring the sweetness of the moment.

He moved away. "But that's a promise for later. When you are ready."

She had no idea what to say.

He touched her cheek and smiled as they walked down the hall hand in hand.

24

She sat in the sanctuary, staring at the lit-up cross.

"Angelina." The voice was soft, almost a whisper.

She startled.

Cooper touched her on the shoulder. "Sorry, didn't mean to scare you. I saw you slip in here after the meeting. I thought you might want to talk. I know it's been a rough few days. Nate told me what happened with the little boy."

She scooted down on the pew to make room for him. "I am exhausted."

He sat down. "Of course you are. From what Nate told me, it was the wee early hours before either of you left the station this morning."

"It's more than that. I just…I just don't feel strong enough to do this. Any of this."

"What do you mean?"

"I want to get better. Get healthy. Really, I do, but I'm not strong enough. Every time I think I'm getting stronger, something happens to make me fall apart. Again."

"You don't have to be strong enough. All you have to do is rely on God. He's strong enough when our own strength fails us. He wants us to depend on Him."

"I wish I had your faith." She looked over at Cooper. "But I don't. I think that's part of the problem. I wasn't healthy before Luther Marks. I can see that now. All I cared about was partying and being famous.

I was so selfish and self-centered."

"Did you know that the mustard seed is the tiniest of seeds?"

Several comments came to mind. He'd obviously slipped off on a tangent. "No, I didn't."

"It is. But when it matures, it's huge. Almost like a tree."

"Oh." She still had no idea what he was talking about. "That's nice."

"Nice? That's more than nice, that's wonderful."

"OK."

He started laughing. "You have no idea what I'm talking about, do you?"

"Not really."

"But I do have your attention now."

"That you do."

"Good. So here's my mini-sermon for the day. Matthew 17:20 says, 'If you have faith as small as a mustard seed, you can say to this mountain, Move from here to there, and it will move. Nothing will be impossible for you.'"

"Nothing? Do you believe that?"

"Some days, I don't feel that way, but I know it's true because it's in the Bible. The point I'm trying to make is we don't need a whole lot of faith to get started on the journey or even to keep moving. Just like the mustard seed, faith grows as it matures."

"Oh. So a little bit of faith is all we need?"

"Exactly. Our faith grows as we see that God is truly faithful. And I know you have faith that's as least the size of a mustard seed."

"How do you know that?"

"Because you're sitting here, staring at the cross. Remember our talk about sowing and reaping?"

She nodded.

"Faith is the same way. Keep sowing faith and you'll reap the harvest of more than enough faith when you need it the most."

"That might be true for you. You're a good person but..." She took a deep breath. "But I'm not. I've done...so..."

He patted her arm. "We all have, Angelina. You're not in the minority there. I could shock you with things from my past. And God has forgiven every one of them. And He will do the same for you."

"I don't know about that."

"I do. He loves you just as much as He loves me. And that's where faith comes in. When we know that God loves us, we can trust Him."

She sat there thinking about his words. Could that be true? Could it be that simple? "So what do I need to do to make my faith seed grow larger?"

"From where I'm sitting, you're already doing it. You seem to be reconnecting with God. And you're trying to focus on other people, not just yourself. That's two of the biggies."

"It is?"

"It is. Mark twelve thirty says, 'Love the Lord your God with all your heart, and with all your soul, and with all your mind, and with all your strength.' It goes on to say to love your neighbor as yourself. So as you learn more about God, you'll love Him more. And you're already showing that you love others. Why else would you have risked so much for Charlie and his mother? So you see you're well on your way."

"Wow. Who knew?"

"Keep studying the Bible and you'll get there. It's all about..." He pointed at her.

"Baby steps." She smiled. "I guess you're right. I need to be a little more patient with myself."

"I'd say a lot more patient, but that's usually true for all of us." He patted her arm as she stood. "Glad I could help. Stay as long as you want. We don't lock the church. And by the way, sleep really does make things better. Taking care of yourself physically is just as important as spiritually."

"Thanks. See you Sunday." That would be a huge step, one she was ready to take. She smiled. Definitely a step in the right direction.

~*~

Angelina stepped out of the church into complete darkness and froze. The parking lot light must have burned out. "Luther's not out there in the dark waiting for me. Or anyone else. He can't hurt anyone ever again." After taking a determined breath, she forced herself to move away from the safety of the church. Her footsteps clicked on the sidewalk as she hurried to her car. Why had she stayed so late?

Everyone else was long gone. But the time she'd spent in the church had been worthwhile. She felt stronger and more committed to getting her life on the right track. There was a lightness in her being that had been missing for a long time.

She touched her lips, remembering the warmth of Nate's kiss. He'd called it a promise. She knew with God, she could get healthy. Be the type of woman Nate would respect. Even love?

With God's help, Luther wouldn't win. She would

be whole.

Angelina stared at her lone car in the parking lot. Why hadn't she parked closer? She took a deep breath and kept walking. Behind her, footsteps echoed. She froze. *Just my imagination, just as with Luther's voice.* She moved forward. And heard the footsteps-again. Too terrified not to look, she steeled her nerves as she turned and peered into the darkness.

No one was there.

Her pulse spiked as her imagination kicked into overdrive. Telling herself to relax, she kept walking toward the car. Nobody was following her. Nobody wanted to hurt her. There were no footsteps. The sounds weren't real. Only her imagination gone wild. But she took hold of her pepper spray, just in case.

More footsteps echoed around the lot.

Fear made her want to crumble right where she stood, but she wouldn't. Her finger moved to the spray button as she turned, ready to stop them. No one was there.

Impossible, she'd heard those footsteps. Someone was following her. It wasn't her imagination. He was there. Just because she couldn't see them—him, didn't mean he wasn't hanging around. He was waiting for her. He was back just as he'd promised. She'd never be free of him. Luther was making good on his word. Even if she couldn't see them—him.

It wasn't her imagination.

He was real. Luther wanted to hurt her. To do things to her—again. She would rather die than let that happen again.

Angelina reined in her panic. Luther was dead, so it couldn't be him. If not him, then who?

Shivers ran down her back as her breath turned

ragged. She kept walking. The car—gotta get to the car.

The footsteps continued to pound the lot's tarmac.

This time she didn't look. She fished the keys out of her coat pocket. Her finger moved to the button on the pepper spray. She'd be ready this time. It wouldn't happen to her again. She wouldn't let it.

God help me.

As Angelina sprinted the last few steps to her car, she hit the remote's unlock button. Closing the distance, her hand reached for the handle. She opened it in a swift movement. Without wasting a second, she jumped in and pressed the lock button. In spite of the blood pounding in her ears, she heard the click of the doors. Safe. After a couple of deep breaths, she chanced a look at the parking lot.

Empty.

How had he managed to hide? Maybe he was kneeling right beside her car. She wouldn't be able to see him there. But he was somewhere. He had to be. It wasn't her imagination. Those footsteps had been real. Someone was following her. Someone was after her.

She'd heard many times—once a victim always a victim. Something about the way a person projected themselves made them a target. Not her. She was done being a victim—with God's help.

Her hand shook as she put the key in the ignition. Taking a deep breath, she started the car and drove out of the parking lot. Looking in the rearview mirror, there was still no one to be seen. The parking lot was empty as far as she could tell. Of course, with no light it was hard to see.

The hairs on the back of her neck tingled.

Breathing. Someone was in the car perhaps hiding behind the front seats. The sound was unmistakable.

Quiet, but rhythmic.

Angelina fought back the terror that threatened to overwhelm her. *Stay calm.* Focus on figuring out how to get out of the car alive. She'd been in such a hurry to get to safety, she hadn't looked in the back seat. How could she have forgotten something that important? Every woman had been taught since childhood to check the backseat before getting into a car. Especially at night.

In spite of her attempts not to panic, her breathing turned to short gasps.

What was she supposed to do now? She couldn't just jump out of the car. He'd catch her in a heartbeat. No doubt, he was stronger and faster than she was and prepared to pounce.

If she wanted to survive, she had to act as if everything was normal—until she got to some place safe. She had to act as if she had no clue. Lull him into a false sense of security so he'd wait until she got home before attacking her.

He might be stronger, but she was smarter. Smart always won. At least that's what her dad had always told her. Angelina turned on the radio, hoping to drown out the sound of his breathing. But she could still hear it.

The torment continued.

Finally, the bright lights of a gas station came into view. Perfect. She quickly pulled into the parking lot, jumping out of the car the moment she slammed the gear shift into park. Her gaze immediately moved to the backseat.

Empty.

Impossible. How could that be? She'd heard his breathing. Practically felt his breath on her neck.

Angelina opened the back door and leaned in to make sure the backseat was as empty as the front. Then she moved to the trunk. Might as well make sure he wasn't there either.

Empty again.

That was good—and bad. Good because she was safe and bad because...her eyes filled with tears. Her imagination had won again. It all felt so real—too real. She didn't want to get back in the car. Even though her eyes told her it was perfectly safe, it wasn't. No place was safe. Luther would never let her be safe. He was after her again—even if she couldn't see him.

But that was impossible, Luther was dead. He couldn't hurt—

"Hey, are you all right?" A man walked closer. "Having car trouble?"

Angelina stepped back. "I'm...I'm fine. I...just thought I heard something in my car."

"Want me to take a listen? I'm a pretty good mechanic if I say so myself." His gaze raked over her body.

Her stomach tightened. "No. No. No. Everything looks OK. Must have been my imagination."

"You sure? I don't mind."

She managed a nod.

"Maybe you want to go get a drink or something?" He arched his brows at her in a playful way.

"I can't." She mumbled as she slid in the car and locked the doors. As she drove out, she checked her rearview mirror.

The man still stood there staring after her.

Was he the one following her?

Angelina forced her breathing to slow down.

He was somewhere in this car with her—even if

she couldn't find him.

She pushed harder on the gas. Had to get home. Had to find someplace safe. But where? It didn't matter. No place was safe. He would always find her.

No place was safe.

Angelina pulled into the drive. Instead of heading toward the garage, she maneuvered her car between the cement posts and drove up the brick sidewalk toward the main house. She dashed up the steps, refusing to think about who or what might be lurking out there in the darkness.

She banged on the door as she pushed the buzzer. "Hurry, Keren. Hurry. Let me in." Still hitting the buzzer, she turned back toward the car.

He couldn't pounce without her seeing him coming.

Nobody was there.

The door opened. She lost her balance and fell inside.

"What's wrong? Are you OK?" Keren's voice rose.

She wasn't OK. She fought back tears. "I...I...don't want to talk about it."

"You have to tell me what's wrong or I can't help you." Keren's face flushed red. "We're family. And I thought we were friends."

"You have to take care of your rich, crazy cousin because she can't take care of herself."

"Please don't say that. We love sharing our life with you. We're family. Families take care of each other." Keren reached down and pulled her up. "Come on. Sit down in a chair and relax. I'll get—"

"Can't." Angelina pulled away from her. "He's...he's back. He followed me. In the car...breathing...I heard it." She swiped at the tears making their way down her cheeks. Her knees began to shake.

"Who's following you?"

"Luther."

"He's not following you. Angelina. He's dead. He can't hurt you anymore."

"Maybe…he had a partner. It was dark in that basement. I don't know. Could have been more than one of them. No one ever thought about that. He promised to make me pay. I…I heard him breathing in the car."

"It was just your imagination. That's all. You need to calm down."

"Not my imagination. I heard him." Her voice rose with each word. "I know what I heard. He's in my car."

"Do you want me to go check?"

"No. I already did. I couldn't find him."

"You're not making any sense. You tell me he's in the car, and then you tell me he's not. You need to calm down. Tell me what happened tonight to get you so upset."

"It might not make sense, but I know what I know. I heard the footsteps, but every time I turned around, nobody was there. I heard him breathing in the car."

"Well, it was probably dark and spooky in the parking lot. That happens to all of us sometimes. Our imaginations can make us think cra…make us think things. That's all it was."

Angelina had to make Keren understand. "Once I was in the car someone was in there with me. I even stopped at a gas station. I expected to see someone crouching in the backseat but no one was there."

"You're just stressed. After all you went through

last night, I'm not surprised. I knew you weren't strong enough to handle all this. And now you're getting stressed and…and I just think it might be too much."

"It's him. He's following me. Why won't you believe me?"

"When did you go off your meds?"

"I didn't. I take them every morning. Just like I'm supposed to."

"Are you sure you didn't forget a day or something? If you were taking your meds—"

"You don't believe me. You think I'm getting sick again. I'm not sick. I heard him breathing in the car. He's back, and he's following me. You have to listen to me." Sobs started as she slid down the door and to the floor. "You have to believe me. You have to help me."

25

Nate looked up as someone knocked on his door. Bonnie Wright.

He stood as he motioned for her to come in. "What are you doing here? Is Charlie OK? Is it...safe for you to be here? They haven't taken him from you, have they?"

"No." She shook her head. "We're safe enough for now. Thanks to all of you they think it was a case of mistaken identity. Angelina's lawyers are in the process of getting our social security numbers changed to match our new names. Bonnie Wright and Charles Wright. Hopefully, they'll never know how close they came to finding their grandson."

"I'll be praying for that. What can I do for you today?"

She shook her head. "I...I'm not sure how to explain this, but Charlie insisted I come talk to you."

"About what?"

"He's worried about his Miss Angelina."

"Why?"

"He says there are ghosts in her house, and he wants the good policeman, that's you, to chase them out of her house. He says she's not safe with the ghosts in her house."

Dumbfounded, Nate stared. "I'm not sure what to say to that. But, of course, to calm his fears, tell him I'll go look for the ghosts. And if I find any, I'll definitely chase them out of Miss Angelina's apartment."

"I know it's silly but he was so worried, I had to promise to talk to you before he would agree to go to school today."

"He's back in school?"

"I wanted to keep things as much the same as possible. The psychologist said it would be good for him. Angelina's paying for that as well. Plus, she's working on getting me a new job. She's so kind and so amazing."

He couldn't agree more about Angelina, but he wasn't ready to share his feelings about her with others just yet. "So how's the lawyer working out?"

"She is so...so good. She promises everything is getting taken care of. That we will be able to live like normal people again. Angelina has been so good to us."

"That's sounds just like Angelina." Maybe, he'd call her up for another one of their doughnut dates. She'd been so anxious last night that she hadn't spoken a word during the meeting except a little social chatting. She'd gone into the sanctuary afterward. He'd wanted to follow but felt it wasn't the right time.

He didn't want to intrude on her spiritual journey. But he did want to make sure she was OK. Besides she'd enjoy the story about Charlie being worried about her and the ghosts in her apartment. It would make her smile.

He wanted to be the one to make her smile. Even though she wasn't quite ready for that sort of a relationship yet. Nate pushed the thought away and focused on Bonnie. "I'm glad things are working out so well for you."

She smiled. "Well, I must go. I'm on my break

from the restaurant. I wanted to talk to you before I see Charlie again so I can put his mind at ease. A promise is a promise."

Her words made him think about his promise to Angelina. He'd wanted much more than the sweet kiss he'd given her. He smiled at Bonnie. "You do that. And you know what? Tell him to stop in to see me sometime. He seems like a nice kid."

The other officers were staring at her and then back at his office.

He hoped they didn't get the wrong idea about the two of them. After all, she was a very pretty woman. He picked up his phone and sent a text to Angelina asking if she was hungry for a doughnut. No response. Maybe she was busy.

He picked up the next form that needed his attention. An hour later, the paperwork was finished and he still hadn't heard from Angelina. He picked up the phone and called. No answer. That was unusual. She always answered his calls and texts.

Maybe she was getting some much needed rest. She'd get back to him.

"I want to see Chief Nate." A small voice broke his concentration as he sorted through a computer database. He stood up and walked out to the main room.

Charlie was in the squad room. His mother stood behind him.

"Hey, Charlie."

Charlie waved and ran around the desk to him. "Hi.

"How was school?"

"It was OK."

"Want to see my office?"

Charlie nodded and ran through the door.

Bonnie walked into the station. "He insisted on coming to see you. Had to make sure you chased the ghosts out of Miss Angelina's."

Charlie sat in the chair behind his desk.

"Hey, that's where the chief sits."

Charlie swallowed hard and started to get out of the chair.

"Just kidding. You can sit there. How's it feel? Think you might want to be a policeman one of these days?"

"Yeah. Then I can help people, too. Did you help Miss Angelina? Did you chase the ghosts out of her house?" His eyes were wide and innocent.

Instead of answering his question, Nate asked one of his own. "What makes you think there are ghosts in her house?"

"Because I heard them."

"You heard them? When was that?"

"That night we were at her house. Mama made me go to bed so she could talk to Miss Angelina. About adult things."

"And you heard the ghosts?"

He nodded.

"What did they say?"

"The ghost kept saying, 'Ange. Ange, do you want to play?' And then it'd say 'Come play a game with me, Ange.'"

Nate's gut twisted and his blood ran cold. No way Charlie could know those were the same words Luther Marks had used when he'd terrorized Angelina in the basement.

Nate looked over at Bonnie. "Did he tell you that?"

"No. He just told me she had ghosts in her house."

"Did you see anyone in the room, Charlie?"

"No, silly. You can't see ghosts. They're in...in...you know you can't see them."

"Did they say anything else?"

"Yea..." He rubbed his little hands together as he thought. "Something about not getting away. He would always be around. I don't know. Something like that."

Angelina had claimed she'd heard Luther's voice the night she'd jumped out the window. Dr. Markley, Keren, even Nate had thought she'd been dreaming. Apparently, they were all wrong. Someone was still out to get Angelina.

"I'm really glad you told me about these ghosts, Charlie. You did good. You'll make a good policeman someday."

Charlie jumped up out of his chair. "You got to help her."

Nate stood. "You're right. I do need to help her. And that's exactly what I'll do. Right now."

Fifteen minutes later, he drove up to Angelina's garage. When he tried to enter it was locked. He pressed the doorbell then the intercom. No response from either of them. He looked up toward the main house. Angelina's car was pulled up in front of it. On the sidewalk. Maybe she was in visiting with Keren.

As Nate walked up the steps to the house, the door opened.

Keren stood there, not smiling. "What do you want, Chief Goodman?"

"I came to see Angelina."

"You're always coming to see Angelina. What for this time?"

"She's not answering my phone calls or my texts."

"Maybe you should take a hint then. She's not interested."

"Angelina and I are friends, Keren. Where is she? Why's her car parked out front like that? I haven't seen her do that before."

Keren rolled her eyes and shook her head. Her voice lowered a notch or two. "I don't think I should be telling you anything. Angelina's business is Angelina's."

He refused to take her hint. "What's that mean?"

"It means what it means. I know you're only trying to help, but Dr. Markley says we shouldn't push her. She'll heal on her own schedule. Trying to make her do more than she's ready to do will only add stress, and she doesn't need that."

"You think I add stress to her life?"

"Yes. You got her involved with that kid, and then you made her go to that meeting last night when she was quite clearly not wanting to go. If you hadn't shown up, she wouldn't have gone."

"I was only trying to help her."

"Look, I know you're just being nice but she doesn't need that kind of stress."

"So where is she? I really need to talk to her. I'm not leaving until I make sure she's OK."

She shook her head and moved aside.

He walked inside.

Keren motioned toward the stairs.

He couldn't help making a comparison between this grand circular staircase and the simple stairs at Keren's previous house.

"She's upstairs resting."

A woman walked down the steps. "I'm all done. And I was very quiet as you asked. I made sure I didn't disturb her. See you next week."

"Thanks, Marta." The woman left. Keren looked at him. "She's the cleaner."

Angelina had told him she'd signed with a landscaping service and had hired Peter to take care of the house and the grounds since he'd lost his job. And now a housekeeper. So Keren and Peter got to live here for free and get paid. Perhaps they didn't want to change the cushy life they'd come into.

This is her family, Goodman. He hated being a suspicious cop at times. "So what's going on? Why is Angelina here instead of her own apartment?"

"She had a little episode last night so she stayed here. She was too afraid to go back to her apartment."

"Afraid of what?"

"I really don't think she'd want me telling you. But...Luther Marks. She was convinced that he was chasing her last night. That he was in the car with her. She was really freaking out."

"Is she OK now? What did Dr. Markley say?"

"She wouldn't let me call her. She's been up in her room all day. I figured she'd come down when she was ready. She'd probably feel better after she got some sleep."

That's what he'd thought, too. Until Carlos told him about the ghosts.

"I'm going up to see her." He started up the stairs and then turned back to Keren. "Unless that's a problem?"

She shrugged. "That's fine. I know she trusts you. Hopefully, she won't be mad at me for letting you in." She walked past him and led the way. At the top of the steps, she pointed at a door. "That's her room."

"Thanks."

"No problem. If she gets mad at me and kicks me out, I'll come stay with you." She laughed. "Just kidding. She wouldn't do that. Angelina really has changed so much since...well, you know since that." She walked down the steps.

He knocked on the door.

No answer. Was she sleeping? Maybe she was, but she might just be hiding out from the world. He opened the door. The room was empty. "Angelina. It's Nate."

Nothing.

He walked over to another door in the room and knocked, "Angelina, are you in there?"

Nothing.

"You'd better be decent because I'm coming in." He opened the door to a lavish bathroom, complete with a separate shower and a spa-style tub. Empty. He walked back in the room and went to the windows. They were all locked. She hadn't left that way. Feeling slightly silly, he checked under the bed, and then the closet, the largest one he'd ever seen. It was almost as large as his whole bedroom.

No Angelina. He walked to the doorway and called down the steps. "Keren. She's not here."

Keren ran up the steps. "What do you mean she's not here? Of course, she is. Angelina. Angelina." Keren repeated the action he'd just performed—except for looking under the bed. "I don't understand. Where is she?"

"When was the last time you saw her?"

"Last night. She was so upset so I gave her something to calm her down, and then I helped her to bed. When she didn't get up this morning, I just figured she was still asleep."

"But that was hours ago?"

"I thought she was too embarrassed to come down and needed some time to get herself together. I didn't want to bother her. I was trying to give her some space."

"And what? You thought she'd stay up here all day without anything to eat or drink?"

She pointed outside the room. "I brought her up some breakfast. The tray's right outside the door. I didn't see a reason to bring up lunch since she hadn't eaten breakfast yet. And it's not like the room is tiny. It's a suite of rooms, as you can see."

He bit his lip and counted to ten. There was logic in what Keren was saying. "Could she have gone back to her own apartment without you noticing?"

"I suppose so. It's a big house, and there's more than one way out. And it's not like she's a prisoner. She's even told me to stop hovering over her so much. That's what I was trying to do. Give her some privacy."

"She didn't answer when I was at the apartment a few minutes ago." He thought of the ghosts Charlie had heard. Nate didn't believe in ghosts, but he did believe in evil.

26

"Why are you doing this?" Angelina's eyes were open. But it didn't matter. She couldn't see a thing. She was surrounded by complete darkness. How had this happened to her again?

"I thought you might want to play a game with me." The whispered response echoed around the room.

This had to be a nightmare. Luther Marks was dead. Leslie had shot him. But her eyes were open. She wasn't asleep. This was real. A sharp jab to the bottom of her foot proved that. She tried to move her foot away but couldn't. It was tied to something. She was pretty sure it was a bedpost. Had she never left Luther's basement?

Maybe Nate rescuing her had been the dream—a fantasy. Could her mind have made that whole thing up? Dr. Markley, Charlie–Carlos, Rosie, and Fred wouldn't be real either. She'd gone crazy and made up a bunch of people to keep her company. What was that called when one heard voices and had people inside their head? There was a name for it. And she was still a prisoner trapped in Luther's basement, on top of her craziness.

She screamed into the darkness. "Leave me alone."

"I want to play." The whisper had moved. Now a sharp jab in her arm. A moment later one on her leg—the other side. "Don't you like to play with me, Ange?"

"My name is Angelina." She yelled. Her grip on reality was slipping. If she lost it, she might never find herself again. She called out in the darkness. "God, help me."

"God can't help you. Only I can."

Not true. God was real. The faith of a mustard seed. That's all she needed. That's it. Focus on God. I can do all things with Christ who strengthens me. One of the Bible verses from the group.

The group had to be real. She hadn't known that verse before the group. If the group was real, so was her rescue. And so was Nate, dear, sweet Nate. She remembered the warmth, the tenderness of Nate's kiss—his promise.

Nate was real.

Charlie-Carlos was real.

And if all that was real then Luther Marks was dead.

And that meant someone else was doing this to her.

"I want to play, Ange."

Another sharp jab and then the knife scraped down her left thigh. The sharp pain probably meant she was bleeding. *Stay in reality. Don't slip away.* "Who are you? You are not Luther. He's dead. Luther is dead." She repeated it over and over, denying this person's faking being Luther.

Laughter, then the room was flooded with light.

A man stood near her. He wore a hood and he had a knife in his hand. The one he'd been jabbing her with. Blood dripped on the blade. Her blood. "You're right. Luther's dead. I was just messing with you. I thought maybe you'd freak out and forget," he still whispered.

She'd been right. She was tied to a bed and still

had her own clothes on from last night. Though his knife had obviously cut through the leg of her pants. She glared at him. "Who are you? What do you want? Why are you doing this to me?"

"So many questions, but not to worry. I really don't want much. Not much at all." He held up a paper then whispered, "I just want you to sign this little paper, and then I'll be on my merry way."

She must not have heard him correctly. Sign some paper? That didn't make sense. "You were in my car last night, weren't you?"

He laughed. "Was I? Did you see me there, Ange? You told Luther he could have your money. I'm just holding you to your word. That's all." He waved the paper at her. "I get the money, and you get to live. I think it's a good deal, don't you? Win-win."

Her gaze moved down from the paper to the hand that held it. And then she knew who the monster was.

~*~

"I went to her apartment before I came here. She didn't answer when I was there a few minutes ago," Nate said as they walked outside.

"Maybe she didn't want to talk to you. I keep trying to tell you she's not interested in you, but you won't leave her alone. You keep pestering her."

Ignoring her statement, he pointed at her car. "Why is her car here?"

"She was very upset last night. I already told you that."

"What upset her?"

"She got very confused. Thought Luther was chasing her again. She was sure he was in her car with her."

"And you didn't think that warranted a call to Dr. Markley."

"She told me not to. I was respecting her wishes."

"We need to check her apartment. See if she's there." His stomach clenched as he pictured what he might find there. This was his fault. He should have seen that the incident with Carlos had put her under too much stress. But she'd seemed fine. "What else did she say?"

"She said Luther had been talking to her every night. Asking her to play his sick little games. I wanted her to talk to Dr. Markley about it, but she said it would go away soon. Just like yours did." Her accusation was clear. Keren believed this was his fault.

He stopped walking and stared at her. Those were the same words that Charlie's ghosts had spoken. Someone was playing games with her mind. But who was it and what did they want?

~*~

Angelina gasped as she saw the tip of the tattoo peeking out from his sleeve.

"What's wrong with you?"

She knew who the man was. But if he knew she knew, he'd kill her. She quickly moved her gaze up to the masked face, not wanting him to know what she'd seen. She screamed at him. "I'm in pain. You hurt me, remember?"

"Sorry. I didn't want to hurt you, but I had to let you know I meant business." He moved closer. "You do know that, right? This is not a game. It's deadly serious. There's no reason for you to have all that money. It's not fair."

Her eyes focused on the wall behind him. When he moved, she saw the Diamond logo. She was somewhere in the Diamond plant. That meant there had to be people around. People who could help her. Maybe if she screamed...

As if reading her mind, he whispered, "Don't bother screaming. Nobody'll hear you. Don't you think I would have taped your mouth if that was the case? I'm not stupid. All you'll accomplish by screaming is to make me angry." He held up the knife. "And that's not a good idea."

The air in her lungs deflated.

"So you won't mind signing this paper, right?"

"Right. If I sign it, you'll let me go? That's what you said."

"That's the deal."

She nodded. "Then I'll sign it." She prayed it would buy her some time.

"Good girl."

He untied her one hand then handed her a pen. He put the paper on the clipboard and moved it closer. Her gaze scanned the paper and found the words, *Last Will and Testament*. This was his get-rich scheme. If she signed it, it would be like signing her death warrant. But what choice did she have? Her hand shook as the pen touched the paper.

"And make sure it's the right signature or you'll be sorry," he whispered, his voice still threatening.

She signed her legal name.

He pulled the paper away and stared down at it. "Good girl."

A moment later she was plunged into darkness once again. "You promised you'd let me go. You promised."

The only response was a door slamming.

~*~

After hitting security buttons to get in the garage, they both ran up the steps to Angelina's apartment. Again, Keren hit the buttons.

He dreaded opening the door, not sure what he would find.

It sounded as if she'd had a complete psychotic break last night. And if that was the case, who knew what she might have done.

But the apartment was empty.

He breathed a sigh of relief.

"If she's not here, where is she?" Keren looked at him. "I don't understand."

Before he could answer, Nate's phone rang. The station. "Chief Goodman."

"Nate, this is Rene. I just got a strange phone call. It's probably a prank, but I thought I'd better tell you about it."

"What?"

"The voice said, 'She's at the Diamond plant.' Then he hung up. I tried calling back, but there was no answer. He didn't say who *she* was. You think it was a prank?"

His heart sank. "No prank. Send backup to meet

me at the Diamond plant. Now."

"What's going on?" Rene asked.

"No time, just tell them to meet me there. And that it's an emergency." He ended the call and looked at Keren. "I think I know where she is. Gotta go."

"I'm coming, too."

"No, you're not. You're staying here just in case she returns. You call me the minute that happens." He took the steps from the apartment two at a time. Keren was right behind him.

"I think I—"

He turned toward her. "Please, you stay here. I need to know if she comes back or if you hear from her."

"OK. Fine."

Peter walked across the lawn. "What's going on?"

Keren ran to him. "I'm not sure. Angelina's gone. She might—you tell him Nate."

"Don't have time. You fill him in." With those words, he ran to his cruiser.

Two other cruisers sat in the Diamond parking lot. The officers stood together. They both jogged up to his cruiser as he stepped out "What's going on, Chief?

Nate stepped out of his car. "I know it sounds crazy. But I think Angelina Matthews is being held against her will somewhere in the Diamond plant."

"You mean, like, kidnapped? Again? That does sound crazy. You think that's what the phone call was about?"

"Kidnapped twice? That's really bad." The other officer shook his head in disbelief.

Nate nodded. "I think the phone call was about Angelina, I was at her house when Rene called me, and her cousin doesn't know where she is. Her car is there, but no one's seen her since last night. I'm betting she's in there. Somewhere." His gaze moved to the factory.

"Let's go find out."

The three of them walked inside.

Nate walked up the receptionist. "Hey, Mary. How are you?"

"Fine, Nate. What's going on?"

"I need to talk to the plant manager. Now. It's an emergency."

"Sure thing." She rushed over to the door. After knocking, she stuck her head in. "The Chief of Police is here, Stanley. Says it's an emergency."

Stanley walked out, and so did Fred.

"Fred, what are you doing here?"

"I work here now, remember?"

Nate had arrested Fred before. Fred swore his life of crime was over now that he'd found God, but it was so easy to slip back into old habits. Could he have something to do with Angelina being missing? Another one of his get-rich schemes?

His gaze met Fred's. The innocence could be an act. "Fred, if you know what's going on, you need to tell me right now. Before this thing goes any further."

"What are you talking about, Nate? It sounds as if you're accusing me of something."

"I want to know the truth, Fred. Is this another one of your get-rich schemes?"

"I really don't know what you're talking about." Fred sounded sincere enough. Was he being truthful?

Nate didn't have time to think it through right now. He looked at Stanley. "I received a phone tip that someone is being held here against their will. At the Diamond plant."

Stanley's eyes bulged and his mouth moved

without him actually speaking. "What are you talking about?"

"This is confidential. Angelina Matthews appears to be missing. Possibly kidnapped. We received a phone tip saying she was here. We need to check out the place."

Fred looked at Nate. "I didn't do anything, Nate. Really. Whatever's going on, it's not me."

Nate nodded, hoping that was true. "Stanley, do we have your permission to search the property?"

Stanley wrung his hands together. "Of course. Of course."

"We don't have a search warrant."

"I don't care about that. Just go find her."

"Are you sure, Stanley? Maybe you should check with a lawyer first. To be on the safe side," Fred said.

Nate glared at Fred. "Really? That's your advice. Not to give permission for us to look for Angelina."

"Just thinking of the company."

Stanley walked between the two men. "Nate, I'm sure. Just go find her."

The door opened, and Peter rushed in. "Keren told me what was going on. I'm here to help in any way I can."

Nate started to argue but changed his mind. The more people looking, the better. He nodded. "Fine, let's split up into pairs. I'll go with Stanley. Jack, you pair up with Peter. And Scott...I guess you'll have to go alone."

"No, he won't." Mary walked up to the group "I can help. I know the place as well as anyone."

"What about me?" Fred asked.

"I figured since you just started you probably don't know your way around too well."

"That's true, but I'll tag along with you. I'm sure I can manage."

Stanley walked over to a cupboard. "I've got walkie-talkies. We don't use them much anymore thanks to cell phones. But this way we can keep in touch with each other."

"Great idea." Nate said. "Fred, you can stay with me."

After a quick lesson in how to use the walkie-talkies, the three groups separated

From Nate's own days of working here, the basement would be the best place to hide her. But it would also be the hardest to get her in without being seen since the plant ran three shifts. To accomplish that, it would have to be someone with access to the building all the time.

"Stanley, you got keys on you?"

He held up a key ring. "Sure thing."

"We'll start in the basement. Mary and Scott, you check this floor. Peter and Jack, start checking the outbuildings."

Once they were in the basement, they started a room by room search. Twenty minutes later, the three men looked at each other.

"She's not down here." Nate's heart sank. She had to be here, somewhere. Probably terrified, maybe deep in a psychotic break.

When they got back up to the office area, Peter and Jack were still checking out the other part of the building.

Nate looked at the others. "We need to think this through. If Angelina really is here, where would be the easiest place to hide her? It couldn't be down in the basement or this part of the plant at all. It would be too easy for someone to see her when she was brought in. There is a night guard."

"Maybe the night guard's involved," Scott said.

"Why would the night guard want to kidnap Angelina?" Fred sounded confused.

"Because lots of employees hate their bosses. And fantasize about getting back at them."

"What's that got to do with Angelina?"

"Angelina owns this place. Didn't you know that?" Peter sounded as confused as Fred. "I'd think you'd know who your boss is."

Fred looked at Nate. "Angelina's the owner? Of the Diamond plant?"

Nate nodded, wondering if Fred's confusion was real or an act. "It wouldn't be easy to get her down here and keep her quiet. But why would we get a tip that she was here?"

"I have no idea. None of this makes any sense. Why would anyone even want to hurt Angelina?" Mary asked.

The only answer Nate could come up with was money. People got kidnapped for money all the time. And Fred was great at coming up with get-rich schemes. And great at getting arrested for them, as well. If that man had done something to hurt Angelina, Nate would make sure he paid for it.

Peter and Jack walked in. The look on their faces said they hadn't found Angelina either. Mary tapped her finger on the desk. "This is bad. The poor thing's been through enough with that Luther Marks man. Why would someone do this to her again?"

Somebody had wanted to keep her scared, confused. But why? To make it easier to get what they wanted from her, of course. And that had to be about the money. Nate felt it in his bones.

"We've checked everywhere. I don't know where else to look for her." Stanley looked at Nate. "Do you have any other ideas?"

"What about that old building at the other end of the parking lot?" Fred asked. "I noticed it when I came in the back way this morning."

"We didn't check that when we were outside," Jack said. "I didn't even think about the old guard shack."

"It's been closed for years. Since we built the new building," Mary said.

That would be an easy place to get to without being seen. Interesting that Fred was the one who'd suggested it. It wasn't looking good for him. But that would have to wait until later. Right now, he had to find Angelina. Alive.

"Good idea, Fred. Let's go." He was already heading out the door. He jogged through the parking lot with Fred beside him.

Everyone else followed at a slower pace.

As they neared the building, Nate became convinced Angelina was in it.

Someone had placed a huge tarp over it. It was probably as dark as Luther's basement.

Nate knelt down, slipped under the tarp and turned the door knob. It wouldn't open. He pounded on the door. "Angelina? Are you in there?" He put his ear to the door but couldn't hear anything. "Anybody got a key for it?"

Fred slid under the tarp. "I don't think I do. I can look."

"Forget about the key. Let's see if we can open it. Are you ready?"

Fred nodded and leaned his shoulder against the door. Nate did the same. When Nate nodded, they both pushed with all their strength. The old wood door gave way.

The others pulled the tarp off of the building.

Angelina was tied on a bed, just the way she'd been with Luther. Except she had her clothes on. Rage flowed through him. What kind of monster would make her relive that nightmare? He rushed to her side. "Angelina. Angelina."

Her eyes flickered then opened. "Nate. Are you really here? Or just in my dreams?"

He caressed her cheek. "I'm really here, sweet Angelina. And you're fine. It's not a dream."

Fred untied her legs as Nate untied her arms.

By the time they were finishing, Angelina was sobbing. Her arms went around his neck. She whispered in his ear. "Don't leave me. Don't leave me. He'll kill me if you do."

"I'm not leaving you." He turned to the group.

Peter came forward. "Angelina, are you OK?"

She trembled as her arms tightened around Nate's neck. "Fine. I'm fine."

"Who did this to you?" Fred asked.

"Don't know. They had a mask on."

"We better call an ambulance," Fred said.

"I don't need an ambu—"

"Forget an ambulance. I'll drive her," Peter said. "But first I need to call Keren. She's beside herself with worry."

"No." Her voice was loud enough that everyone stared at her. "I don't...need an ambulance. I want to..." She stopped talking as if she had no idea what to do. She still clung to Nate. Again, she whispered.

"Don't leave me. I need to talk to you alone."

"OK, everyone out. Let's give her a minute to get herself together."

"I should stay. I'm family," Peter said. "She shouldn't be alone right now."

"She's not alone. She's with me," Nate told him as the others moved out of the building.

"Fine." Peter looked at Angelina. "I'll be right outside if you need me."

Peter walked out.

Angelina clung to Nate and whispered into his ear. She was still talking when someone yelled, "Bomb!"

27

"Bomb. Boss, get out of that building now?" Jack yelled from outside the building. "Get out. Now. Everyone else move away from the building."

Without another word, Nate scooped Angelina up from the bed and jogged out.

In his arms, she felt safe. She blinked against the brightness of the sun.

Everyone ran across the field. Jack ran up to them. "It looks like some kind of homemade bomb that didn't work. Apparently, they didn't want her getting out of that building aliv—" He stopped talking and looked at Angelina. "Sorry."

"That's OK. I sort of figured that out already."

Nate sat Angelina down but held on to her. "I have an idea."

She listened. When he was finished talking, he looked at her. "Are you OK? Can you do this?"

She nodded. "I can do all things through Christ who strengthens me."

Nate grinned. "Sounds about right."

Peter pulled up in his car and jumped out. "Angelina, you really need to get to the hospital."

She moved away from Nate. He squeezed her fingers one last time as they slipped away.

"It was you. You did this to me." She ran directly to Fred and slapped him.

Fred stepped backward. "What are—?"

"Don't even try to deny it. I know it was you." She pushed at him. "Did you think I wouldn't recognize your voice? Even if you were whispering."

"I didn't—"

"Liar." She lunged at him, screaming. "I can't believe you did this to me. And after I got you this job. I tried to help you."

One of the policemen grabbed her arm and moved her away.

Nate stepped up. "Are you sure about this, Angelina?"

She nodded as tears streamed down her face.

Nate turned to Fred. "You have the right to remain silent…" When he finished, he walked behind Fred and clicked on the handcuffs.

"Nate. I didn't do this. She's just confused. You've got to believe me."

"Sorry, buddy. You just couldn't resist one more get-rich scheme, could you? You're under arrest."

"No. No. You don't know what you're doing. I didn't do anything. I'm innocent."

"Yeah, just like the other times I arrested you. You're the one who suggested she was in that building. How'd you know that? Because you're the one who put her in here." Nate glared. "I'd love to show you what I really think of you but I can't."

Grabbing his arm, Nate pulled Fred toward the two officers and away from the group. Nate had a whispered conference with them out of ear range.

Fred stared at her.

She felt sick to her stomach, but she glared back at him.

Finally, the officer led Fred away.

The other one walked back with Nate, a confused

look on his face.

Nate was by her side in the next moment, his arm touched her. Everything would be all right. Nate wouldn't let anything happen to her. This would all be over soon. Nate looked at her. "How are you feeling? OK?"

She nodded. "A little shaky."

Peter stepped up and hugged her. "I'll take you home."

"No...I don't think so. I want to...I need to see Dr. Markley. Right now. Nate, will you drive me there?"

"Of course. If that's what you want. I'll be glad to do that."

"I can do that," Peter offered.

"No, you need to go tell Keren I'm fine. I'll...I hope I'll be home later. But maybe Dr. Markley will have other plans. I...just don't know. I'm so..." Her words trailed off, and she leaned against Nate as if overcome.

"Are you sure? I don't mind taking you."

"No. Nate can take me."

Peter looked as if he wanted to say more, but then he nodded. "If you say so."

"Jack, you stay here until the sheriff's department comes to process the scene."

"Yes, sir."

Nate's arm went around Angelina. They walked to the cruiser together.

The rest of them still stood in the parking lot, looking shell-shocked.

As they drove away, she looked over at Nate with a smile. "Did I do good?"

"Perfect. Now, let's go finish setting that trap."

"And see who we catch."

"I hate to ask you again, but are you absolutely sure it was Peter in the shed with you?"

"Unless someone else has a tattoo of Keren on their wrist, spelled K-E-R-E-N." Spelling her cousin's name brought tears to her eyes. "Thank you for doing it this way, Nate. I have to know the truth. I have to know if Keren's involved or not."

He reached over and patted her hand. "I understand completely. I'd want to know that too if it was my family."

"Why didn't he just kill me after I signed?"

"I can't tell you what's in his mind, but I'm guessing he thought that rigged-up bomb would do the trick. He had it on a timer and then made sure he would be with witnesses when it happened so that no one would suspect it was him. Then he could pop up with the will he forced you to sign."

"Makes sense. Do you think Keren was in on it?"

"I really don't know, Angelina. She seems to really care about you, but how could Peter have gotten you out of the house without her knowing about it?" He didn't mention that Keren had never liked him at all.

"How will we prove whether Keren was involved for sure?"

"I'm thinking their conversations should tell us what we need to know. If she's involved they'll be talking about it. If they don't talk about it, I'd say she's in the clear."

"That makes sense. How will we do that?"

Nate held up his cell phone. "No time for a bug. I'll hide this in the kitchen for now. I'll get a few more bugs set up by the end of the day. In the meantime, you stay in the living room so they have to go to the kitchen to talk privately."

"Got it. What will you do?"

"After I get the phone in the kitchen, I'll check out your apartment. See if I can find those ghosts."

They pulled into the drive. Her car was still in the same spot from the night before.

She looked at Nate. "My car probably has some sort of recorder or player in it. That's probably how I heard him breathing. And the footsteps."

"And the voice in your apartment as well. I'll check it out. But first let's get in the house before he does. We want to throw him off his game."

"You can park behind the garage. He shouldn't be able to see the car there."

The two of them walked up the steps, hand in hand. She squeezed his. "Thanks."

"My pleasure. I want to get this all behind you, too. I want you healthy so I can keep that promise." He winked.

Remembering his kiss, she leaned against him. "Sounds like a plan."

Before she could press the doorbell, the door opened. Keren squealed. "Angelina. Are you OK? What happened? Where were you?"

"Didn't Peter call you?"

"Peter? Why? Was he with you?"

"Let's go in the house, ladies." Nate herded them in.

"Let's talk in the living room," Angelina said. "Nate, would you mind getting me some water?"

"Not at all." He walked away.

She couldn't break down now. She had to know the truth. Had Keren been involved? Her heart said no, but her mind said maybe. "I was kidnapped."

Keren's eyes grew wide and her face paled. "What

are you talking about?"

"I'm not quite sure what happened, but I woke up tied to a bed today in complete darkness. Just the way I was in Luther's basement. It turned out I was at the Diamond plant. In an old guard shack."

Keren's hand flew to her mouth. She looked horrified. "Just like before?"

"But it's over. They arrested someone."

Keren looked as if she might pass out. From guilt? Her voice was a whisper when she asked, "Who was it? Who did that to you?"

Before she could answer, the door opened.

"Keren? Are you home?"

"In here, Peter."

He walked in. His mouth dropped open as he stared at Angelina. "I thought you were going to see Dr. Markley."

"I changed my mind. I wanted to come home. Be with my family."

Keren hugged her as she said the words.

Please don't let Keren be involved.

He smiled. "Are you feeling better?"

She nodded. "Peter helped find me."

"I'm confused. How did you know what was going on? How did you end up at the Diamond plant, Peter?" Keren asked.

"You told me that's where Nate was going. I wanted to help."

"I did? I don't remember that."

Strike one.

"Probably because you were so upset about Angelina being missing."

"I guess."

Nate walked back in the room with a bottle of

water. "Here you go, Angelina."

Peter paled. "Didn't know you were here, Nate." His voice was shaky.

Strike two.

"Just getting some water for Angelina."

"I'd think you'd have a ton to do at the crime scene."

"Not at all. It's not my crime scene. That's the county."

He nodded. "OK. Well, if everyone's all right, I've got things to do." He turned to leave the room.

"Like what, Peter?" Keren's voice turned shrill. "Angelina just got home from being kidnapped. We need to make sure she's safe. That she's all right."

"She's safe. She's here. I don't know what you want me to do." Peter looked over at her. "Of course, if you want me to stay that's fine. I don't have anything that pressing to do."

"No need," Angelina said. "I'll be fine."

"Yeah, I need to go, too." Nate winked at her. "But first, I'm checking your car and your apartment for tape recorders or mp3 players."

"Why on earth would you need to do that?" Keren's eyes widened.

Peter's eyes flitted from Nate to her to Keren. He seemed ready to hyperventilate.

Nate looked at her. "Didn't you tell her, Angelina?"

She shook her head. "Not yet. I didn't have time. We think someone's been gaslighting me. Right, Nate. That's the right term?"

"What do you mean?"

"I didn't have bad dreams or hallucinations. We're pretty sure someone planted devices to make me think

I was hallucinating. To make me think I was having a nervous breakdown."

She glanced at Peter. He looked like a deer caught in the headlights of an upcoming car.

"That's an awful thing." Keren was appalled. Either that or she was the best actress Angelina had ever seen.

"Why don't you go with me, Peter? Out to her car?"

He blinked. "Well, I need to—"

"Need to what? You go help him. There's nothing more important than proving that this guy was out to hurt Angelina." Keren looked at her. "Who did you say got arrested?"

"Some guy from my support group."

"You're kidding. Unbelievable. I knew that place wasn't any good for you." She glared at Nate as if it was his fault.

"Let's go check out the car, Peter," Nate said.

"Me, too." Angelina smiled at Peter. "I want to see it for myself."

Nate slipped on a latex glove that he pulled from a pocket then opened her car door. He felt under the passenger seat. He held up the prize. "This looks like the culprit." He pressed a button.

Breathing. And then the voice asking, "Do you want to play a game with me, Ange?"

Keren squinted at the media player. "Peter, that looks just like yours. It even has that scratch I put on it. I—" She stopped speaking as if suddenly realizing what that meant. "Peter?"

"Shut up, Keren. Don't say another word."

Strike three.

"I don't understand." Keren shook her head.

"What did you do?"

"Peter's the one who kidnapped me. Not the man from my group."

Keren's gaze flew first to Angelina, and then to her husband. "Peter? That can't be true."

"I saw his arm with your name tattooed on it," Angelina told her. "His sleeve slipped when he was taunting me."

Keren turned to Peter. "Is that true? Why? Angelina's been so kind to us." Her voice broke and tears streamed down her face. "Look at all she's done for us."

"Kind? Throwing us a few crumbs like we're dogs. While she had the whole cake. It wasn't fair. We deserved some of that money."

And you're out.

Keren covered her mouth with her hand, her expression melting into horror. "Oh…I'm so sorry, Angelina. I…I didn't know." She crumpled to the ground, sobbing. "I'm so sorry, I'm so sorry…"

Angelina's heart lifted from the heavy pall of mistrust.

Keren hadn't known.

And that was all Angelina needed to know.

28

Angelina sat in a chaise lounge chair on the deck of her childhood home, alone and in the dark. The stars were twinkling against a velvet black night. Beautiful. She took a deep breath, glad that she could appreciate the beauty of the night again.

For the moment, she and Keren were staying together in the house. Just the way a family was supposed to do. They would get through this together. Keren was devastated, completely stricken by what her husband had done to Angelina. She'd tried to leave, but Angelina wouldn't hear of it. Keren would need a lot of support to get through this, and Angelina planned to be there through every step.

Hopefully, Peter would forego a trial, but at the moment, he was still insisting he wasn't guilty, despite the evidence. Which meant a trial.

Angelina was strong enough to handle it—with God's help. Which was amazing. She definitely wasn't the same person who'd been trapped in Luther Marks' basement. Somewhere in the past few days, she'd gotten un-trapped. All those baby steps had taken her to the right place. The place she wanted to be.

Helping others really worked. It didn't make sense but she was finding out that was true about a lot of things in God's Kingdom. Now, she had to help Keren, who'd given so much to help her.

Her gaze moved up to the night sky once again.

Thousands of stars twinkled to remind her that God was still God and that He loved her. And His love was enough, no matter the circumstances. "I don't know what will happen. But I want You with me on the journey. With You, all things are possible," she whispered into the heavens.

The stars seemed to twinkle brighter for a few seconds as if God was agreeing with her. She sat in the chair staring into the night sky, savoring the feeling of complete peace, even in the midst of the storm she'd been in the past few days. She heard a rustling and then footsteps. But instead of being afraid, she leaned forward, eager to see who the steps belonged to.

"Hey, Angelina." Nate walked up the back steps of the deck. "What's going on?"

"Just sitting here and enjoying the night. It's a beautiful night, don't you think?"

He arched a brow. "I thought you were afr—didn't like the dark."

"Things change." She shrugged as she scooted down on the chaise lounge, making room for him. "I wasn't sure if you'd come or not."

"Are you kidding me? After you left me such a mysterious message to meet you on your deck after dark, how could I resist? So why exactly are you sitting out here in the dark?"

"Two reasons, actually."

He sat down beside her. "That sounds intriguing. Do tell."

"First, I wanted to prove I wasn't afraid of the dark anymore."

"You don't have to prove anything to me."

She looked over at him with a smile. "I wasn't trying to prove it to you. That was for me."

"Oh. Makes sense. So did you prove it to yourself?"

"I think I did. Something feels different. Inside me. Sometime in the past few days, my stopwatch started ticking again. I'm not trapped in Luther Marks' basement."

"That's terrific news." His hand touched hers.

"There might still be some setbacks, but I'm ready."

"Ready for what?"

Her pulse quickened. "That brings me to my second reason for being out here."

He smiled. "What's that?"

"Before I tell you, I want you to know that God's a part of my journey now, and that won't change. Ever. So…" She shrugged, her courage was failing. "I…I just wanted you to know that before I tell the other part."

"That sounds pretty good to me. What's the other part?"

She scooted closer to him. "I think I've made a giant leap forward to the healthy me. And I'm ready."

"Ready for what?" He leaned closer.

She smiled. "For you to keep your promise."

Their lips touched. She closed her eyes, savoring the moment.

They parted.

"How's that for a promise kept?" Nate asked as he touched her cheek.

"Not bad, but I think we can do better."

A Devotional Moment

So don't be afraid; you are worth more than many sparrows. ~ Matthew 10:31

Fear is a double-edged sword. Being scared stops some from fulfilling their dreams, their purpose, and their full potential. But fright can also be caused by others who seek to harm. When one is trapped within the evil intent of another, it can be difficult to break free. Surrounded by distress, pain, and fear, one can feel heart-wrenchingly alone. Evildoers may claim that their victim is unworthy, unlovable, has no value. But that is not true. God loves, values, and believes in us all. With His help we can overcome fear, no matter what the circumstances, whether it is fear to overcome our own issues, or fear from another. God can release us from the chains that hold us back from achieving our goals.

In **Trapped,** the protagonist is in fear for her life. While alone, she has time to reflect that she has not used her God-given talents or lived up to the potential of all she could be. When she is freed, she discovers that she is still trapped in fear. Her captor haunts her, but her sins haunt her even more.

*Have you ever felt trapped and alone—even in
the midst of family, friends and coworkers? It can
be depressing and debilitating. But, did you know
that through the power of the Most High God,
you have the ability to free yourself from fear? It
takes an act of the mind and the will. It might not
be easy, but whenever you're in a situation that
has you feeling trapped and alone, remind
yourself that God loves you, values you and will
never forsake you. The very fact that you can
draw your next breath is proof that you are not
forsaken or undervalued. And because of that,
you have no reason to fear or to feel trapped in a
situation that is out of your control.*

LORD, FREE ME FROM MY SIN AND HELP ME TO USE
THE TALENTS YOU HAVE PROVIDED AND ACHIEVE
THE PURPOSE THAT YOU HAVE CHOSEN FOR ME.
GIVE ME COURAGE AND STRENGTH TO MOVE
FORWARD IN FAITH. IN JESUS' NAME I PRAY, AMEN.

Thank you

for purchasing this Harbourlight title. For other inspirational stories, please visit our on-line bookstore at www.pelicanbookgroup.com.

For questions or more information, contact us at customer@pelicanbookgroup.com.

Harbourlight Books
The Beacon in Christian Fiction™
an imprint of Pelican Book Group
www.pelicanbookgroup.com

Connect with Us
www.facebook.com/Pelicanbookgroup
www.twitter.com/pelicanbookgrp

To receive news and specials, subscribe to our bulletin
http://pelink.us/bulletin

May God's glory shine through
this inspirational work of fiction.

AMDG

You Can Help!

At Pelican Book Group it is our mission to entertain readers with fiction that uplifts the Gospel. It is our privilege to spend time with you awhile as you read our stories.

We believe you can help us to bring Christ into the lives of people across the globe. And you don't have to open your wallet or even leave your house!

Here are 3 simple things you can do to help us bring illuminating fiction™ to people everywhere.

1) If you enjoyed this book, write a positive review. Post it at online retailers and websites where readers gather. And share your review with us at reviews@pelicanbookgroup.com (this does give us permission to reprint your review in whole or in part.)

2) If you enjoyed this book, recommend it to a friend in person, at a book club or on social media.

3) If you have suggestions on how we can improve or expand our selection, let us know. We value your opinion. Use the contact form on our web site or e-mail us at customer@pelicanbookgroup.com

God Can Help!

Are you in need? The Almighty can do great things for you. Holy is His Name! He has mercy in every generation. He can lift up the lowly and accomplish all things. Reach out today.

Do not fear: I am with you; do not be anxious: I am your God. I will strengthen you, I will help you, I will uphold you with my victorious right hand.

~Isaiah 41:10 (NAB)

We pray daily, and we especially pray for everyone connected to Pelican Book Group—that includes you! If you have a specific need, we welcome the opportunity to pray for you. Share your needs or praise reports at http://pelink.us/pray4us

Free Book Offer

We're looking for booklovers like you to partner with us! Join our team of influencers today and periodically receive free eBooks and exclusive offers.

For more information
Visit http://pelicanbookgroup.com/booklovers